"Fans of *Serafina and the Black Cloak* (2015) will find much the same chills and sequel-primed mystery here."

—*Kirkus Reviews* on *Shadow Weaver*

"Vivid and invigorating."

—*School Library Journal* on *Shadow Weaver*

"Connolly's narrative is full of meaningful moral lessons—on the limits of loyalty, the importance of honesty, and the absolute necessity of trusting others…an enchanting new juvenile fantasy series."

—*Foreword Reviews* on *Shadow Weaver*

"This book contains plenty of action and intrigue to keep the reader turning pages. It is quick to read and contains enough unsolved mysteries to make the reader look forward to the next title in the series."

—*School Library Connection* on *Shadow Weaver*

"The theme of friendship is handled deftly here… A gripping finale reveals the truth about the 'cure' for magic, and readers will eagerly anticipate learning more in a promised sequel."

—*Bulletin of the Center for Children's Books* on *Shadow Weaver*

LOST ISLAND

LOST ISLAND

MARCYKATE CONNOLLY

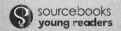
sourcebooks
young readers

Copyright © 2021 by MarcyKate Connolly
Cover and internal design © 2021 by Sourcebooks
Cover artwork © Manuel Šumberac

Sourcebooks Young Readers and the colophon are registered trademarks of Sourcebooks.

Published by Sourcebooks Young Readers, an imprint of Sourcebooks Kids
P.O. Box 4410, Naperville, Illinois 60567-4410
(630) 961-3900
sourcebookskids.com

Library of Congress Cataloging-in-Publication data is on file with the publisher.

Source of Production: Maple Press, York, Pennsylvania, United States of America
Date of Production: August 2021
Run Number: 5022668

Printed and bound in the United States of America.
MA 10 9 8 7 6 5 4 3 2 1

For those who itch to wander

THE LEGEND OF THE LOST ISLAND

It was a time of heroes and magic, when the comet-blessed shared their talents freely and without reservation. A party of young heroes traveled the three territories, learning all they could about magic and wisdom to bring that knowledge back to their beloved home village.

Their water wisher communed with every lake and river and waterfall in the lands, learning how the shape of the terrain had shifted and molded over the centuries. How mountains had risen and fallen, the valleys had been carved between them, and of a time when the sea had risen so high that it had taken over the whole region.

Their gift giver connected with the magic of every talented person they met on their journey, discovering how each one worked. Some who had obnoxious talents like stench summoners or spider callers, begged her to replace them with more useful magic. She graciously bestowed talents to help them and their communities, leaving a swath of green growers and water wishers in her wake.

Their soul summoner visited graveyards and burial grounds, raising the souls of the wisest people who had ever walked the three territories so he could obtain their lost wisdom. He learned their stories, their histories, a depth of understanding never before held by any one person in all the land.

When the trio of heroes had gained all the knowledge they could hold, they finally began the journey back to their village with the full expectation of a triumphant return. Instead they were greeted by disaster.

While they were abroad, a wicked villainess had descended on their village casting a shadow over the three lands. She was a magic eater set on devouring every talent in her path no matter how powerful or insignificant. When the villagers welcomed her, they merely believed her to be a rich traveler with a glamorous entourage. She charmed every one of them, disarming any suspicions they may have had. The tradespeople adored her, for she spent lavishly on their wares during her visit. The elite of the village wished for her favor and vied for an invitation to her grand estate. She remained in the village for one week, ferreting out every talented person, for there were many.

When the villainess departed, she took every last one of them with her. Whether it was by choice or by force, the few remaining villagers did not know. She had been as charming as ever the evening before, and when they woke, she and two-thirds of their townsfolk had vanished into thin air. Those who gave chase either came back empty-handed or never returned at all.

This was the state of the village when our heroes arrived—mourning for their stolen loved ones. They discovered too late from a neighboring village of the rumors surrounding a fine lady who wished to collect all the magic in the territories and hoard it for herself. When the heroes discovered the remains of their village, they mourned along with the untalented villagers. The water wisher cried bitterly for three nights and three days. Her tears flooded her house, then the village, and soon even the lands beyond it until the entire valley was filled with the waters of a saltwater lake.

Their village was forever buried in a watery grave, and grief and fear drove the survivors to leave it behind. The heroes and their friends were determined that their talents must never fall into the hands of the villainess. They set sail across the ocean into the promise of the unknown and were never heard from again.

CHAPTER ONE

Two weeks ago, I found my mother. And then I lost her again.

My mother, Maeve, is out there, searching for the means to raise the souls of her lost children—a sister and brother I never knew I had—and to return power to a dark force that must never rise again.

I can't let her do either of those things. The price is too high.

When my best friend, Sebastian, and I first met Maeve, we had no idea she was both my mother and possessed the body walking talent we so feared. Even my talent for reading minds failed to reveal that until it was too late. We thought Maeve was our friend and protector, helping us look for my vanished hometown of Wren. But all along, she was on her own mission. She used her talent to take over some of our other friends including Sebastian's older sister, Jemma. All so she could use their bodies as hosts for her lost children once she finds a soul summoner.

The only bright side is that we managed to rescue most of our friends, sending Maeve on the run and putting a damper on her plans.

I've long wished to find some trace of my home, my family, but the discovery that Maeve is my mother was bittersweet, tainted by her betrayal.

The Parillan Archives, the library fortress where I've been staying with Sebastian and Jemma, is high in the mountains. The old gray stone walls are thick and solid, but it isn't as safe as it looks from the outside.

Maeve's talent is body walking, so at any moment she can take over anyone she has touched. Only a piece of obsidian can ward off her magic. So we remain here, in the library, searching for a way to stop my mother from carrying out her wicked plan. Maeve was thrilled to learn I'm her daughter, but that wasn't enough. Her obsession is boundless, and she won't rest until she's raised the rest of our family's souls from the grave.

It feels as though we've hunted through these stacks a hundred times, and yet there are still new books and scrolls and maps to uncover. The library is a dizzying sort of endless, one that's hard to focus on. My feet always long to move and wander. Other times I get a bit lost in my own mind. But I have my friends to anchor me and bring me back.

This afternoon I slip away, leaving Sebastian and his sister to the dusty books while I make my way to a section I discovered a few days ago with stories and legends. I find them far more captivating than literal laundry lists kept by town archivists a hundred or more years ago. I locate the book I was reading yesterday, one about the adventures of talented folks—people blessed by the Cerelia Comet with magic—long, long ago. I keep my nose in the book while my legs carry me on a now-familiar circuit of this floor. The other researchers in the Archives have finally ceased sending me odd looks and more or less accepted me as a fixture, albeit a strange one. Except for Connor, a particularly unpleasant man whose mind is as full of himself as it is his research. He still dislikes me as much as ever.

Recently, he went off on a journey of his own, which has been a relief. Those times when I'd lose my grip on my mind reading talent, his thoughts would always startle me back into reality.

The story is intriguing. In it, the heroes have formidable talents and travel across the three territories as disaster strikes their home. When they reach their village, full of news and excitement, they find only the wreckage and a handful of sur-vivors. One of the heroines—a water wisher—cried so bitterly that the surrounding area began to flood until it became a salt-water lake. One of the other heroes was a soul summoner—the very talent Maeve wants most. I'd hoped to learn more about that magic in the story, but to my disappointment it doesn't say much. At the very end, the heroes set sail across the ocean with the survivors, their grief driving them into the promise of the unknown. They were never heard from again. All in all, it's a sad tale, but I've read it twice now and can't help but like it. Rachel, a book binder and the assistant librarian who's been helping us in our search, told me and Sebastian that many of these stories are based on a grain of truth. The trouble is determining which grain is real from all the made-up parts.

Frantic thoughts burst into my head, ripping my attention

away from my book. My talent has wandered again. Panic washes over me. I toss the book aside and hurry out into the hall just in time to see Natasha and Kalia—an illusion crafter and dream eater—dash down the stairs.

"What's going on?" I call after them. Natasha pauses, breathless. Her fancy gown (no doubt one of her illusions) floats around her frame.

"It's Connor. He's back, and he's injured," she says.

Kalia's mouth is set in a hard line. "We overheard two of the librarians gossiping about it. The villagers brought him here in the middle of the night."

My two friends exchange a nervous glance. "They said they think it had something to do with the body walker," Natasha says.

My spine goes rigid. As much as I hate to think it, I can't put that past Maeve. She despises him about as much as he hates us. "But where are you going?"

"We're headed to the infirmary," Kalia says. "I'm going to take his dreams and see if there's a hint of what happened. He hasn't regained consciousness yet."

I haven't seen Kalia's talent in action very often. She once told me Lady Aisling, her former master, used to have her stay up all night in her room and devour any bad dreams that formed in her mind. Kalia hated it. Apparently bad dreams leave a foul taste behind.

"I'll join you. Maybe I can help too," I say, and together we hurry toward the lower tier of the fortress.

When we get to the infirmary, we find the door open just a crack. We huddle near the door, straining to see into the room or hear the doctor, Olga. She bustles around a bed for a minute or two, muttering, then begins to approach. Natasha quickly crafts an illusion to conceal us as we flatten ourselves against the wall, making it look like we're not there at all. We hold our breath as Olga walks out, but she doesn't see us. As soon as she turns a corner, Kalia lunges for the door before it closes completely, and we all creep inside.

Kalia tiptoes over to Connor's bedside and perches on the edge. He mumbles and twitches, but when she places a hand on his forehead, he stills. She's removed a nightmare or two from me in the past, and it has always had a calming effect. It must do the same for Connor.

My talent wanders into his head, but his mind is unconscious and clear now that Kalia has taken his dreams.

"What was he dreaming about?" Natasha whispers.

Kalia's face is drawn. "He found Maeve. But I can't tell where exactly. Somewhere in the woods, but that could be anywhere really. He was so sure he could simply overpower her or outwit her and get back that journal she took from him."

Natasha snorts. "Is that really why he left the Archives?"

Kalia nods.

"That was very silly of him," I say, shaking my head. I knew Connor was foolish, but clearly underestimated how foolish.

"So what happened to him? How did he get hurt?" Natasha asks.

"As soon as he got near Maeve, she used her talent on him. You know he refused to wear an obsidian amulet. The rest of the dream is a strange jumble. Mostly it's just overwhelming powerlessness while the world flashes by at odd angles." She frowns. "It's awfully confusing actually."

"That almost sounds like he was falling," I say.

Natasha gasps quietly. "Maybe she took him over, then threw him down a hill."

My friends both shudder, and my heart sinks. Natasha might just be right.

"Whatever she did," Kalia says, glancing back at Connor as we leave the room before Olga returns, "we don't want the same to happen to us."

That is something we can all agree on.

Later I join Sebastian and Jemma at dinnertime, unable to shake the uneasiness that has followed me since I learned about what happened to Connor. Sebastian's hair is dusty, and he sneezes every so often, which makes me laugh.

This evening, Devynne, the youngest of the researchers, sits at our dinner table. She loves to talk, though after Maeve's betrayal she's backed off on her insistence that we let her interview us about our talents. But she always loves to hear what we've been up to in our research. Word about Connor has spread quickly through the library, so tonight both Sebastian and I find Devynne's questioning a welcome distraction from our worried thoughts.

"Did you find anything interesting today, Simone? Sebastian?"

Sebastian sneezes yet again and wipes his nose. "Not really. More of the same. The few town records from Wren that we found all date from before Lady Aisling arrived and stole all the talented folks who lived there. We can't find anything from after that point."

Jemma puts a hand on his shoulder. "Well, we're not done looking yet. If there's more here, we'll find it. Rachel's been a great help."

Maeve won't hurt my family again if I have anything to say about it, she thinks.

Once, Jemma's assurances were fearful, but after our adventures, she has become braver and more determined. She understands me and Sebastian a little better too, now that she's tasted a hint of what we experienced for years.

"What about you, Simone?" Devynne turns her attention to me. "I saw you wandering with your nose stuck in a book half the afternoon. It must've been interesting."

I push a green bean around on my plate with my fork while I dip into her mind for a moment. Her thoughts are merely excitable, not teasing or unkind.

"It wasn't research. Just a story. I found a book of legends.

It holds my interest a little better than town records." My cheeks warm. I know I need to remain focused so we can stop Maeve. What happened to Connor has only made that clearer. I may not like him very much, but no one deserves to be treated like that. "I suppose I needed a little break."

Devynne nods. "Perfectly understandable. Stories capture the imagination in the best of ways. They can be refreshing. What was it about?"

"Well, I liked it because there was a soul summoner in it."

Suddenly the others at the table sit up straighter. Devynne's eyes glimmer. "Do go on."

"There were several heroes with talents. One of them was a soul summoner, just like Maeve is searching for. They traveled for a long time and had all sorts of adventures, but when they arrived home, they found their village had been destroyed. The water wisher cried so hard it flooded the land as far as the eye could see, then they and the handful of survivors took one last journey to the ocean and sailed away never to be seen again."

Sebastian frowns. "That's a terrible story. Too sad."

"I liked it," I say, slightly offended. "It reminded me of what happened to Wren."

Devynne's eyes are keen and sparkling. "Simone, you may have stumbled upon a clue to what happened to your village."

"But it's not in any of the town archives. It's just a story, not history. Not a fact," I say.

Devynne smiles. "Sometimes the line between the two is very thin. Especially when talented folk are involved."

My breath catches. "Wait…you think it might really be based on that?"

"Well, you've been wondering why it flooded and what happened to the other villagers. There were no rivers nearby nor any other good reason for it to flood. The work of a water wisher, however, would make perfect sense." Devynne pauses, putting a finger to her chin. "In fact…that brings something to mind."

"It does? But what?"

Sebastian practically vibrates beside me, his mind brimming over with excitement.

Devynne gets to her feet and smiles. "Meet me in the library when you're finished with dinner. Third level. I think I have something to show you."

With that, she hurries away, leaving me overwhelmed by a mix of confusion and curiosity.

CHAPTER TWO

We've gathered around a table in the ancient manuscript room, made from the trunk of an enormous tree. The book with the legend has been passed around, and we've all read it. According to Devynne, there are two versions—one that claims the surviving villagers were never seen again and another that says they left their village behind to sail to a secret island off the coast of Abbacho and have lived there ever since, unfettered by the passage of time.

Devynne swears the second version is somewhere in the library and that it contains more detail that may be helpful in our search. She's looking for it now with Rachel's assistance.

We've hunted through the stack of books Maeve was examining just before her abrupt departure, but so far nothing has connected. In light of the legend, I'm looking through it one more time with Sebastian. Kalia and Natasha are eager to help as well. Maeve captured them and used them with her body walking talent. They feel guilty about the role they played under Maeve's direction, fighting unwillingly against me and Sebastian. And they're very concerned about Melanthe and Elias, our two other friends who are still under Maeve's thrall. Their families agreed that the library is the safest place for Kalia and Natasha. Having them nearby has been both reassuring and strange.

These walls feel tighter and tighter every day. A chain constricting around my chest, making it hard to breathe.

I wasn't made to be trapped like this, stuck in the same place with all these people and loud minds. I need my freedom. I need to roam.

While Maeve is on the loose, I'm not even allowed to wander the woods, though the whispering trees call to me every morning. The sooner we find and stop my mother, the sooner I'll have my freedom back.

Then I can get away from all this deafening noise. My talent has always been a double-edged sword, now more than ever. I do my best to keep my talent in check, so I don't dip into the minds of those around the table, but it's harder than usual. Everyone has a strong opinion, especially after what happened to Connor, which makes their thoughts feel like screams. It's disorienting.

Devynne startles us all as she thumps a thick tome onto the middle of the great table. "I found it."

The book is brown leather, and cobwebs still cling to the spine. Devynne turns to a page near the middle. "We know Maeve has the journal of a soul summoner. Connor managed to find her, but he didn't get it back as he'd hoped. We don't know where it's leading her. This book, however, has an account of a soul summoner and some other rare and powerful talented folks who fled from a village just like Wren to a new home on a distant, secret island long before the formation of the network."

Before the Lady was defeated, many of the talented banded together to form the network. They were a loose web of trustworthy people who helped the comet-blessed move and hide to evade capture. Now that she's defeated, the network isn't as much of a secret, but its members still make great allies.

Devynne points to a passage at the bottom of the page and reads aloud for us.

> The party, mourning the loss of their friends, vowed to never set foot in the three territories again. The new threat was too great, and they feared their talents would also be stolen and used for ill. The best way to ensure the rising evil would never have their powers was to leave. They left their village behind and traveled through Parilla and Abbacho, steering clear of Zinnia, through a treacherous staircase of a mountain range and a dangerous jungle filled with vines that could squeeze the life from a grown man. They finally arrived at a forgotten cove and sailed the rock-spiked ocean to an island paradise. They have never left and never will, determined that their secrets and magic will remain hidden.

"You think this is the trail Maeve is following?" I ask.

Devynne nods excitedly. "I'd bet my entire research project on it. She has the soul summoner's journal. That may very well have clues to the location too."

"But why?" Sebastian asks. "Does she really believe they'd still be alive after all this time?"

Devynne's eyes sparkle. "She has good reason to believe that, actually."

"What do you mean?" Natasha looks just as confused as the rest of us.

"Some talents are so powerful that there can only be one at a time. Like magic eaters, or sky shakers. Soul summoners and gift givers also fall into that category." Devynne pulls the book toward her as she sits in her chair. "There have been no recorded soul summoners or gift givers since the ones from Wren disappeared."

Surprise resonates through everyone at the table. We didn't realize this, but of course Devynne should know. This is just the sort of thing she's researching here at the Archives.

"Please," I say to my friends. "We need to find Maeve. We have a lead now. We must go after her."

Sebastian frowns, his mind a roil of fear. "I don't know. It seems like a big risk without more solid direction." *I don't know if I can handle being taken over again. I'm sorry.* I can feel him quivering, even through his thoughts.

Jemma puts an arm around her brother. "He's right. We don't have a clear path. Just some vague steps. We don't even know if the legend is real. It could be a wild-goose chase."

Kalia gets to her feet. "Simone's right. We must do something. That woman is out there, taking over who knows how many people to get what she wants. If she's successful, we're all in even more trouble."

I nod vigorously. "We can't *not* do something. Every second we remain in hiding is one Maeve is using to get closer to her goal." I wrap my arms around myself. "It's too important. We must act now."

"Let's not be hasty," Jemma says, reaching out for a better look at the book. "This journey sounds very dangerous. And how are we going to get to this island anyway? We don't have a boat."

"We'll figure that out if we can find that cove," Natasha says.

"The legend mentions several landmarks. Maybe we can locate the path on a map," Rachel proposes. She's been silent and pensive so far, which is unusual. She thumbs through a stack of maps on a nearby shelf. Soon she finds what she's looking for and sets a large scroll down in front of us, smoothing out the edges as best she can.

"This is where the library is located." She points to a mountain peak in the center of Parilla. "And here is Lake Uccello, where Wren used to be." She uses her talent to note the starting point of their journey on the map. "Now let's see if there's a mountain range that looks like a staircase...here!" She stabs her finger excitedly at a section with a marking for mountains that does look quite like stairs. It's about halfway between the library and Lake Uccello. "The Plateaus. They're flat on top, so they do look like steps from afar. And then not long after that they would've crossed into Abbacho and entered the jungle there before they could reach the seacoast."

"See? We can head to the Plateaus and try to catch up to Maeve," I say.

"But how are we going to stop her?" Sebastian asks.

We're all silent for a moment.

I take a deep breath. "I can convince her. She's my mother."

The others do not seem persuaded. In fact, I know they're not.

Poor Simone, so trusting in Maeve's goodness. There isn't a shred of it in her, Natasha thinks bitterly. I flinch, yanking my talent out of her head. I hadn't realized it was loose.

Jemma places a hand on my shoulder. "While we can hope you'll succeed in that, we need a better plan. We need something more. She must be stopped." *At all costs…*

"What would you propose?" I ask.

Kalia doesn't hesitate. "The talent taker. We need to send word to the network that his services will be necessary. We'll capture Maeve. Maybe using obsidian somehow? Then we'll take her to him, and he can remove her talent forever."

I shrink back into my chair. This is an argument I've feared—and avoided—for weeks. Removing a talent would be as awful as removing a limb. A violation of the worst sort, reserved only for the most dire of cases. But what a terrible talent body walking is! Should a power like that really be entrusted to anyone? What right have we to decide?

I may question this, but those who've been taken over by Maeve around this table—Sebastian, Jemma, Kalia, and Natasha—have not a single doubt between all four of their minds. The certainty in their thoughts is so hot, it nearly burns.

"How can I agree to do that to my own mother?" I whisper.

Sebastian understands, but he still disagrees. *I'm sorry, Simone. She's too dangerous. We can't trust her.*

"Why don't we take a vote?" Rachel suggests. "First, all in favor of heading out in search of Maeve, raise your hands."

Everyone but Jemma and Sebastian raises their hands immediately, including Rachel. Sebastian looks guiltily between me and Jemma, then shyly raises his hand too.

Thank you, I think at him.

We need each other, he thinks. *Besides, we're a good team.*

"That settles that. Now, all in favor of having the talent taker relieve Maeve of her body walking talent when she's captured, raise your hands." I sit on mine, but every other hand in the room shoots up.

When we find my mother, her fate is sealed.

CHAPTER THREE

The next morning, the clouds burn red as the sun rises over the Archives. I'm not sure if it's a good sign or a bad omen, but we're heading out after Maeve today regardless. Rachel and Devynne stayed up late into the evening charting our route onto a new map that we could take with us. Rachel's book binding talent has more uses than I'd realized, and I'm fascinated by it. The head librarian, Euna, is sending Rachel with us, both to help and to record the journey for the library.

I like Rachel. She's smart and knowledgeable and has a bit of a rebellious streak too. I also know from reading her thoughts that she's one of the few people making this journey who believes I actually have a chance at convincing Maeve to give up her quest.

I've barely spoken to Sebastian since last night, though he has tried to reach out. I'm exhausted already from holding in my talent, and it's only midmorning. Thankfully we'll be leaving very soon.

I grab my small pack of necessities for the journey and take one last look at my room. It's small and quaint, and it's something I was able to call mine for many weeks now. After we stop Maeve, I have no idea what happens next. Will I return here? Will I go home with Sebastian and Jemma? I have no real home, and so far nowhere has quite fit.

But I will miss these walls and many of the people inside them.

I open my door and find Sebastian sitting in the hall with his own bag and a sad expression in his eyes.

"I'm sorry," he says.

"I know," I say simply, closing the door behind me. Some other visitor to the Archives will probably take that room now. I focus on that instead of looking at Sebastian.

"Please don't be angry at how I voted. You know how she terrifies me."

"I'm not angry. Just…disappointed, I suppose." I stare at my hand lingering on the doorknob. "I've always been able to count on you before."

"You *can* count on me. It's Maeve who can't."

My lip quivers and I face my friend. "She's my mother. Hurting her hurts me too."

Sebastian's shoulders slump. "I know, but I'm afraid of her hurting everyone else."

"But mostly you." I regret the words the second they pass my lips, even though they're true. Sebastian looks as though I've struck him.

"You think I'm a coward," he says.

Tears burn in my eyes. "Not a coward…just afraid." How did I just make such a mess? Sebastian has been my anchor, and now that we're on opposite sides it's painful. Especially because it's about family. He knows how much finding my family, my home means to me.

"What's the difference?" He picks up his bag, waiting for an answer.

I don't know what to say.

"I guess we should join the others and get going," he says. Then he walks away.

We join the others at the entrance to the library and say our goodbyes. Euna herself sees us off, and Devynne too. Ida and Connor are absent, though that is no surprise. Ida has never liked us, and Connor is still in the infirmary. But the doctor, Olga, and the cook and many others have gathered to wish us luck.

"We've already sent word to the network. The talent taker will be ready when you need them," Euna says.

"Let's hope we catch her quickly." Jemma's words are met with approval by all. Except me.

We file out into the clearing surrounding the front of the library. The view of the mountains from here is stunning. Below us is all forest and rocks, and we can see as far as the horizon in each direction. The world feels limitless. How will we ever find Maeve in all this?

I briefly let my talent stretch, touching on the minds of my companions as we begin our descent on foot. I quickly discover that everyone, it seems, is avoiding me. No one wants to meet my eyes. Except for Rachel. She smiles at me and helps me up when I trip.

"Steady on, little one."

I smile gratefully, but can't help feeling shaken. These are my friends. Sebastian and Jemma have long been like family. Now none of them want me near. But I can't help clinging to the hope that my mother can be redeemed.

While they may say outwardly that they understand, they can't hide the truth. Their minds betray them.

They blame me, even if they don't want to.

I have no idea how to set this right All I know is we need to find Maeve, and I must convince her to abandon her plan. She's already lost so much; I can't bear the thought of stealing her talent too.

Rachel and Jemma lead the party, chatting and occasionally smiling despite the seriousness of our task. They've become fast friends since Jemma was freed from Maeve's magic and joined us at the Archives. Together, they guide us down the mountain by the safest route and the one nearest the Plateaus. We're headed there first. I've traveled these woods before, but I don't know them nearly as well as Sebastian's home village and the surrounding area. I miss the simple forest there with its maze of gurgling streams. This is much different. The trek downhill on this side is arduous and knotted with roots and rocks that jut out of the earth at odd angles. The trees are thick and plentiful and full of birds and squirrels who watch us as we pass by. I try to focus on their thoughts, simple and curious, but there is no evading the ever-present weight of the minds in this party.

My knee catches on the edge of a rock, and I tumble forward, accidentally shoving into Natasha. She manages to steady herself on a nearby tree, but I end up face-first in the leaf-coated path.

"Are you all right?" Natasha asks, holding out a hand.

A laugh bursts from my lips before I can think better of it, and the sound ricochets strangely off the trees. No one else is laughing; they just stare at me, surprised. I pull my talent in as tightly as I can. I don't want to hear what they think of me now. I can't seem to do anything right.

It's too late for me to rummage through the minds of the local wildlife for a trace of Maeve or her captives, Elias and Melanthe. People have longer memories than animals. Once we reach the first village, I'll have to use my talent on every person we encounter, just in case. I'm only beginning to get my talent back under my own control, and I've been trying so hard not to breach other people's privacy by invading their minds. But it doesn't matter anymore.

Politeness won't help us find my mother.

CHAPTER FOUR

It's late afternoon when I begin to feel the press of many minds through the whispering mountain trees. I tug on Rachel's sleeve.

"We're getting close," I say.

"Oh good, I'm ready to stop for the night," she says. This village lies on the other side of the mountain and near the bottom of another peak in the range.

It isn't long before the trees break and the village appears in the distance beyond a field of wildflowers. A brick wall surrounds it, but we're on high enough terrain that we can peek over and see the little roofs crafted from blue slate on top of houses of all colors and sizes. I hope Maeve only passed through and hasn't troubled them much.

The hum of so many thoughts blend together, a constant buzz in the back of my brain.

The grass growing alongside the flowers comes up to my waist, and I run my hands over it gently. I can't help myself. I spin through the flowers and grass, letting the greenery tickle my skin. For a moment, everything becomes a whirl of green and red and white and blue. Until someone catches my hand and tugs me back onto the path.

Kalia laughs. "This is serious stuff, Simone. We have to stay focused."

Focused. That word has become the bane of my existence. It comes more easily to everyone else. They don't seem to grasp the temptation of flowers or a burbling stream. Or spinning in a sunbeam. It's exhausting to try to do what everyone expects me to do and not what my feet demand.

I know the stakes are high. I know I need to try harder. I have been; it just isn't quite enough.

"Sorry." My face flushes red, and I tuck my hands into the pockets of my skirt.

When we reach the village, we enter the gates to little fan-
fare. The porter is helpful and directs us to the local inn, where
we can find food and rest.

"Thank you for your help, sir," Jemma says. "Might I ask…
Has there been another party of a woman with auburn hair and
two children, strangers to your village, arriving here in the past
few weeks? We have friends who were traveling this way, but we
don't know if they took the same route."

The man's round face lights up. "Yes, actually. There was
a nice woman like that with two kids, a girl and a boy, a couple
weeks ago. They didn't stay for long though. Just a night or two,
if I recall correctly."

"Thank you," she says. "That's helpful."

My stomach flips as we make our way toward the inn.
Maeve was here. She walked these same streets. But at least the
porter looked on her without fear or displeasure. Perhaps she left
this place untouched. For their sake, I hope so.

The inn and tavern are loud and filled with the crush of
many weary minds. We eat a quick dinner and settle with the
innkeeper, a kindly old woman who gives each of us a sweet
after the meal. Then we retire to our rooms, Rachel, Kalia, and

Natasha in one, and Jemma, Sebastian, and myself in another. Sebastian and I settle down on our cots and Jemma on the bed, and we try to get some sleep.

But my mind will not stop whirling, kept alert by the roar of so many thoughts nearby.

Are you awake? Sebastian thinks from across the room.

At first, I don't answer. I'm not sure I want to talk to him right now. But I already miss him.

Yes.

It's good that we're really on Maeve's path, isn't it?

I suppose.

It doesn't seem like she troubled these people. That's a relief, Sebastian thinks.

She isn't a bad person, you know. She's just blinded by her grief, I respond.

That doesn't mean we can let her hurt whoever she wants.

But she isn't. That's my point. She isn't doing anything need-lessly. I squeeze my eyes closed as they begin to burn with unshed tears. *She made me a promise.*

What was it?

That if she could find a way to regain her family and not hurt our friends or anyone else, she'd do it. She promised she'd try to find a way. I think that's what she's doing.

I hope so, Sebastian thinks.

He doesn't have to tell me the rest of what he feels; I already know. He hopes I'm right, but isn't willing to bet on it.

If this was about anyone but my mother, I wouldn't blame him for it either.

It is only the early hours of the morning when I'm awakened by a rustling in our room.

And the feeling of an unexpected mind.

I lay as still as possible, frozen in terror. Then I let my talent loose and probe the mind of the shadowy figure.

I instantly regret it.

I know the mind inside all too well. It's Maeve, but not her body. The sickly feeling of her body walking talent in use turns my stomach. The mind of the woman she's taken over—the inn-keeper, probably, flails deep inside, buried under Maeve's power. All it would have taken is a single touch for Maeve to take her over the first time. And now, she can claim this poor woman anytime she chooses no matter the distance between them.

I must know how much they've discovered...

She's rummaging through our bags. She wants to know if we're onto her plans.

I can't let her do that.

I leap up out of the cot, screaming at the top of my lungs. Jemma startles awake and so does Sebastian. I throw open the curtains, and the moon illuminates the figure. I was right—it is the innkeeper. Her face is slack with surprise, but quickly shifts to that of a cornered animal.

And then, she crumples to the floor.

Maeve is gone. We've seen this before. The effects of her magic will linger. It always happens when she takes over someone who isn't like me or Sebastian. Someone who hasn't already been damaged.

Rachel shoves open the door to our room and gasps at the scene. Kalia and Natasha peer around her, eyes wide and frightened.

"What happened? Why is the innkeeper in here?" Rachel asks, but even as the words leave her mouth, the truth hits her. She shudders and clutches the obsidian necklace she wears.

"Maeve was here," I whisper, confirming everyone's worst fears. "She was looking through our things, trying to piece together what we've guessed of her plans."

Rachel straightens her spine. "Then she was looking in the wrong room. The map and books I brought along with me are in *my* room, safely tucked away in my bag. She won't get near them if I have anything to say about it."

Sebastian frowns. "They allowed you to bring books out of the Archives?" As far as we knew, all books are not allowed to go any farther than the reading tables, let alone out of the building.

Rachel looks uneasy. "'Allow' isn't quite the word I'd use," she says. "I didn't exactly ask permission. But they might be helpful, and we all voted not to waste any more time so...." She shrugs, then sheepishly stares at the floor.

I throw my arms around her waist, surprising her, but earning a smile. She's taken so many risks for us. I don't know how we'll ever repay her.

The innkeeper groans on the floor, drawing our attention. Her eyes are wide and unseeing, the result of the body walker's tampering with her mind. It will fade in a day or two, but the disorientation is awful at first.

"I'll see if I can find her daughter," Kalia says. "They run the inn together. I was chatting with her at dinner tonight." She runs off down the hall.

Jemma is bent over the innkeeper and has placed a pillow underneath the woman's head. The innkeeper's eyes move among the five of us like a fly that can't sit still. Her mouth is slack and she moves her lips as if she wants to say something, but the words just won't come out.

The poor woman. I hope this passes quickly.

I can't bear to look at Sebastian, not after our conversation right before we fell asleep. I want so badly to believe Maeve can change back to a good mother. The mother I believe she must've been once upon a time. But the truth is, I don't really know. My memories of my childhood are long vanished, and all I can hold to is hope.

CHAPTER FIVE

The next morning we leave the inn quickly, after assuring the innkeeper's daughter that her mother's state is not permanent. We also warned her that she and anyone else Maeve came into physical contact with should begin wearing obsidian at all times.

It's a sober reminder of what we're up against: Maeve could've taken over a dozen people, even a hundred, in the last few weeks, just long enough to form that first connection.

She could be watching through anyone's eyes at any moment. And we'd never know.

"What I don't understand," Sebastian says through the muffin he's eating, dropping crumbs on the path, "is how she knew where we were. I know she can take them over once she's done it the first time, but how did she know to take over *that* innkeeper in *that* village? What if she has innkeepers in every village in Parilla?"

Sebastian shudders, and Natasha looks as if she might become ill.

"She very well might," Kalia says, folding her arms over her chest.

"Maybe she got lucky?" I say.

Jemma shivers next to me. "Or maybe she was trying different people all night until she happened upon one who'd seen us recently." She shakes her head. "Now that she knows we're following her, there's no telling what she might do."

"*I* know what she'll do," I say, my expression grim. "She'll keep doing it to stay on our trail. Sooner or later she'll be successful. She'll find out what we know, and then she'll change her course of action so we can't find her."

Rachel swallows hard. "She is very smart. But I'll be guarding those documents that might give away our plans."

"I hope it's enough," Jemma says.

So do I, but with my mother, there's no way to know for certain.

Sebastian tries to send comforting thoughts my way, but I brush them off. I'm too distressed by what happened and too embarrassed to admit I was wrong. His sympathy is the last thing I need right now.

Instead, I do my best to focus on putting one foot in front of the other, watching the terrain gradually shift under my feet. For a time, it helps, and almost keeps me in line. But eventually I drift away, only to be recalled now and then by one of my friends.

By midmorning, we reach the tail of the mountain range where the peaks turn into the Plateaus. They rise above us, their flat tops looking for all the world as if a giant came by and sliced them off long ago. We make our way around the base of the Plateaus, heading for the wooded area that our map says lies on the other side. It will be easier and safer than trying to climb them. Then from there we will head toward the coast.

It is slower going than we'd like, but by late afternoon we reach the edge and can see the forest not far away, as well as a village just beyond a swath of crop fields.

We begin to approach the village, but Jemma pauses, holding her arms out to stop those behind her. I peer around her waist to see what made her halt so suddenly.

"What are they doing?" Sebastian asks in a quavering voice.

A field full of ripe vegetables lies before us, with swollen pumpkins, squash of all colors, and tomatoes. At various spots in the field stand villagers who must've been picking the crop.

Except they're no longer putting vegetables in baskets; they're still and staring—at us.

"I don't know," Jemma whispers. None of us move a muscle. Neither do the villagers. They don't even seem to blink. My hands begin to shake. I know what's happening.

My talent brushes over each of their minds, confirming my worst fears: Maeve is controlling *all* of them.

"We should leave," I whisper. "Maeve has them under her control."

Then, they rush toward us.

"Go!" Rachel cries, pulling Jemma back and pushing us all toward the woods. We don't hesitate. We dash headlong through the forest, following Rachel's lead. Branches crack as our pursuers enter the woods. Ahead of me, Natasha moves her hands, gesturing as she does when she crafts an illusion. Soon there are incredibly realistic illusions of each of us, and she sends them scampering through the woods in the opposite direction.

"That ought to keep them busy for a while," she says with a smile.

Sebastian lets out a nervous laugh, and I can't help but grin. We're lucky to have talented folks on our side.

When we reach the far edge of the forest, all sounds of pursuit have disappeared. We finally slow our pace, much to my relief. I'm shorter than the others, and it's been a struggle for me to keep up.

"I think we've lost them," Jemma says. "That was quick thinking, Natasha."

Our friend ducks her head. We're not accustomed to having our talents appreciated; all we know is having them used. I'm glad Kalia and Natasha are finally experiencing what it's like to be around others who are kind.

"It's getting dark. We should find somewhere to stop and rest for the night," Rachel says.

"Anywhere but that village," Kalia adds with a snort.

"Definitely not," Sebastian agrees.

We press on until we're out of the woods, not wanting to linger there in case Maeve still has those poor people hunting for us. We give the village a wide berth and instead head for the river in the distance.

When we find a spot with some cover inside a ring of boulders, we stop to have a quiet dinner. Everyone is lost in their own thoughts. Except me. I'm lost in theirs.

There must be something here that can help, Rachel thinks as she studies one of the books she brought with her. An undercurrent of fear and frustration fills her.

Why can't we all just be safe again? Jemma thinks as she stares at the bread in her hands. A thing I've often wondered. Why did this have to happen? There are so many questions, whys, and what-ifs that it would be easy to get tangled up in them. I move on to someone else's mind instead.

I miss my mother, Kalia thinks. When we were under the Lady's thumb, Kalia managed to keep her memories of home by the seashore. Even though missing her family caused her pain, I always liked dipping into her mind to see her memories. That remembrance of what it was like to have a family, a normal one, was completely foreign to me.

But she and Natasha are brave. They didn't have to come with us. They could've stayed within those library walls if they'd wanted to, but they chose to come on this journey with us.

Ugh, I'm so tired, Natasha thinks, and I almost laugh. We're all exhausted, it's true. But she's the first to voice it, even if it is only inside her head.

After dinner, we settle onto our bedrolls, and I let my talent roam freely. I'm exhausted from holding it in all day. Sometimes I'm a little jealous of my friends' talents. Sebastian and Kalia can't go around taking memories and dreams accidentally any more than Natasha can inadvertently craft an illusion or Rachel can write a book. My talent is tied directly to my subconscious. It gives me a sixth sense of sorts, but I've never quite figured out how to shut it off.

Regardless, it's hard to fall asleep when I'm worried about reading minds unintentionally, so I've decided to forgive myself for it while I sleep. Usually all I hear are dreams anyway, so it's not too invasive. Sebastian is the only one who knows I do this. I tell him everything. It feels very strange not to have been talking to him much lately. I miss him, but I'm afraid he's mad at me. Or worse, that he's right, and my mother really is unredeemable. Her recent stunts are not helping matters.

So when he reaches out to me in his mind tonight, I hesitate.

Are you awake, Simone?

Yes. I'm awake.

Do you know what Maeve wanted to do with us if she caught us?

I sigh. *She wanted the same thing as last night. To find out what we know. And if we know too much, to stop us from following her. Their heads were filled with one instruction: find and capture.* I shudder under my blanket even though the night air is warm.

She'll do anything to keep us out of her way, won't she?

I bite my lip. *Probably. Except for me. I'm the only one she'd let get close because I'm her daughter. I know her plan is to come for me once this is over. But capturing me while she hunts for the soul summoner would be just as good an option to her, I think.*

A sudden, unexpected ferocity shines clearly in Sebastian's thoughts. *We won't let her take you. I promise.*

I swallow the lump in my throat. *Thanks.*

After that, Sebastian's mind begins to wander and slowly drifts off into dreams. I stay a while in his head, letting his thoughts soothe and comfort me until slumber welcomes me home too.

CHAPTER SIX

Today we follow the river and reach the edge of the jungle, something none of us have seen before. Rachel and Jemma are nervous, their minds full of what-ifs, but we plunge ahead anyway. Tall, wide-leafed trees rise over our heads, and long, clinging vines grasp at my wispy white hair. Colorful bursts of flowers are illuminated by the light slinking its way between the branches. Strange plants with spiked leaves dot the undergrowth, and birdcalls and animal screeches echo over our heads. The hum of insects is an ever-present roar in the background, and the humidity feels like the touch of ghostly hands.

I have never experienced anything like it.

This is a strange new world. It would be easy to get lost here. My feet long to wander down every path we don't take, but my friends keep me in their sights and gently correct me when necessary.

We gawk at our surroundings but press on as best we can. There are a handful of paths where others have gone before us, but no road or even a clear-cut route. Rachel does her best to navigate by the position of the sun and the direction of a thing called a compass which she carries with her (another item she borrowed from the Archives).

Are we safe here? Sebastian thinks at me.

As much as anywhere, I think back. *There are lots of animals, but if any want to eat us, I can redirect them. Remember that time I talked down a bear?*

Sebastian shudders. *I hope we don't have to do that here.*

Me too. But I can if we must. Animals don't scare me much. They can't sneak up on me, because I can feel their minds. Predators' minds are loud when they're hungry. And believe it or not, they can be reasoned with. Why attack a scrawny human girl who'll put up a fight when I can tell them about a more easily acquired snack nearby?

We stop to rest and eat lunch around midday. We've stuck close to the river, and Natasha fills our canteens while we share our food. We've only been on the road a short while, and I'm already tired of beef jerky and cheese. Perhaps tonight we'll be free of the jungle and can find an inn with a good meal and a warm bed. It's a risk but I, for one, am willing to take it.

Natasha returns with the canteens, and I take a deep drink of water from mine. The jungle is humid, and it's harder work walking all morning here than in the more arid places in the three territories. I'm tempted to wander over to the river and dip my toes in to cool off...

"Where are you going?" Kalia says as she catches my hand.

"Oh!" My feet were obeying the whims of my brain before I fully realized it. "It's just so warm, and the river looks so cool..."

Kalia laughs. "Why don't we save bathing for later? If you're tired now, just imagine how much worse it would be walking around the rest of the day in wet clothes."

That's a good point. I'm glad she stopped me.

"Come over here, Simone," Jemma says, patting the ground beside her. "Have some more to eat and rest your legs for a bit. We'll be moving again soon enough."

I do as she says, her presence comforting, though I still worry about whether she and Sebastian are mad at me. What if they don't want me around anymore after this because I defended Maeve? I don't know what I'd do if I lost them. I never wish to find out.

I yawn. The trek through the jungle wore me out more than I realized. I finish my crust of bread, then lean my head on Jemma's shoulder just to close my eyes for a few moments...

This dream is the worst I've ever had. The jungle air is suffocating, constricting around my chest so tightly that I can hardly breathe. Just when I fear I can't take any more, the dream vanishes, and I'm jolted awake.

Hissssssssss.

With a start, I realize I'm no longer on the ground. Instead, I'm up in the branches of the tree we rested under to eat our meal. Through the leaves, I can make out Jemma's form nearby, held fast by dark coils just like the ones around me. Panic slides up my throat, but I swallow it down. Am I still dreaming or is this real?

"Help!" shouts a voice elsewhere in the trees. Kalia. She must've pulled me out of my dream. Did everyone fall asleep?

The sinewy ropes coil up my chest, squeezing harder. I know what has us.

A snake. I've read about such creatures in the library. I've seen garden snakes before, of course, but the jungle variety are supposed to grow to enormous lengths.

Hissssssssss.

Dizziness sweeps over me. They are supposed to be very dangerous too. There are many types, but the most frightening ones are the poisonous kind and the squeezing kind that swallow their prey whole. These must be the squeezing kind. My head throbs.

There's only one thing for me to do.

Though my chest aches, I pry open the snake's mind, hoping to learn more about what it wants and how to convince it to release us.

The snake's mind is full of one thing: hunger. Insatiable, hollow hunger. Desperately I send my magic out into the jungle, hunting for a way to distract the snake with a different creature. There are a couple larger animals near the river, a little way north. I can't quite tell what kind they are, but they appear to be fishing for food in the water.

It squeezes again and I let out a choking cough. My heart pounds so hard I can feel it reverberate throughout my entire body. There isn't time for me use my magic as I normally would. Instead I send images into the snake's thoughts. Ones of a warm, sizable animal with lots of meat on its bones instead of scrawny little me.

My captor arches around to face me. Its beady eyes and scaly skin are terrifying enough, but even worse is the huge mouth that yawns before me as it hisses. The slithering forked tongue and two fangs as big as my arms are the stuff of nightmares. My lungs suddenly refuse to take in air.

Its grip loosens slightly. My talent stretches across the way to where I heard Kalia yell. There's a second snake, and it has a couple of my friends too. I send the same images into its head. Both creatures are unsure about these strange sudden images that have appeared in their minds. But my talent is persuasive, and I build up the animals nearby to be so much tastier and better than us. And little by little the snake's grip relaxes until I'm resting on the ground next to Jemma again.

I don't dare move a muscle until the snakes slither away, which they do only after I send one last sense-thought of how terrible we'd taste.

Kalia rests on the ground across the jungle clearing from me, terror-filled eyes wide and her mouth clamped shut. The minutes tick by, and I follow the minds of the snakes as they give chase to the other animals. I feel guilty about sending them after innocent creatures, but I couldn't let them have me and my friends for dinner. I didn't know what else to do.

"Are they gone?" Kalia whispers.

Yes, I think-speak in her head. She closes her eyes and slumps forward, breathing out in relief.

I look around and realize our friends are all unconscious. *Hurry*, I think to her, *they might be hurt and need our help.* I get to my feet and begin checking Jemma for injury.

But Kalia frowns for a moment then shakes her head. *They're no more hurt than you or me. They're sleeping.*

Sleeping? Through that?

You were too. I had to wake you up. Kalia crouches near Jemma, then frowns deeply. Jemma begins to stir. Not far away, I hear Sebastian and Rachel stir too.

Jemma sits up, confused, rubbing her rib cage. "What's going on?"

We quickly explain as she scrambles to her feet, then hugs a now-awake Sebastian tightly. Rachel joins us.

"Where's Natasha?" Rachel asks.

I could have sworn I saw the flash of her red hair not far from Rachel while I was in the tree, just behind a rock. I run over, hoping against hope that she's all right. I can't feel her mind here anymore, and that makes panic spike in my chest. But there she is, still as if she's sleeping. I reach out to shake her shoulder—and my hand passes right through.

Shocked, I don't move an inch. Sebastian is right behind me and saw everything too.

"It's an illusion," he whispers. He's right. That's why I couldn't feel her mind.

"Natasha's gone," I say.

Rachel's expression grows grim, and she yanks up her pack and paws through it. She groans and casts it aside again.

"So are the books," she says. "Natasha must've taken them."

An awful cold feeling starts in my feet and slowly freezes

its way up my body. There is one explanation that makes sense. The worst situation possible.

"She's back under Maeve's control," I say.

"But how?" Jemma says. "We're all wearing obsidian. Aren't we supposed to be safe from her?"

If we're not safe with obsidian, we're not safe anywhere or with anything, she thinks.

"Perhaps she dropped it while we were running through the forest?" I suggest. Our flight from the villagers was swift but chaotic. It would've been easy for a stone to fall out of a pocket unnoticed until it was too late.

Without a word, we all check that our obsidian talismans are still safely on.

"We need to find her," Rachel says. "Those books belong to the Archives. I must return them. And more important, Maeve can't know what we know."

Kalia snorts. "It's a bit late for that, don't you think? Now that she has Natasha and the books, she knows everything she needs to about our plan."

I wince.

Jemma tugs Sebastian closer to her side. "That, while

unfortunate, doesn't really matter. We need to find Natasha to rescue her from Maeve. We promised her and her parents she'd be safe with us. We owe it to her."

"I agree," Rachel says. "We have a duty to keep everyone on this team together. If it were anyone else, Natasha would be all in for retrieving them too."

Our greatest strength is not our individual talents, but our loyalty to one another. We must protect one another at all costs.

"Then let's go find her," I say.

CHAPTER SEVEN

I send my talent wide, searching the jungle for Natasha's mind—or what I fear I'll actually find: Maeve's talent crushing my friend's will down and using her limbs for her own ends.

I don't find her anywhere. She must be too far away for me to sense. But that's not the only trick I have up my sleeve. I probe the minds of animals in the trees around the place we stopped for lunch. Every monkey and bird and bug. Even those snakes that wanted to eat us. It takes a few minutes, but I finally pick up Natasha's trail thanks to the memories of a small bird with bright-red plumage.

"She went that way," I say, pointing. We waste no time. I

use the animals' minds along the way to ensure we continue in the right direction and adjust our path where she took a turn.

So many questions tumble through my head. I'm no longer sure whether they're my own or my friends. Did Natasha betray us willingly? Or was it Maeve, taking her over? But how? We have no answers, just fear that rests anxiously on all our shoulders.

My legs begin to ache, but we can't stop. We must catch up to her before she reaches Maeve. Trouble is we have no idea where Maeve is hiding now. She could be in another territory entirely or just around the corner. So far, I've only felt her talent in use, not her real mind. I hope she isn't close.

Rachel, I think as loudly as I can. *Do we have more obsidian?* She glances over at me, startled, but takes it in stride. She's still adjusting to being around a mind reader. Not an easy thing, as I know well.

I did procure extra pieces from the jeweler in the village near the Archives when I ordered them to protect the librarians and researchers there. They're in my bag. She pats the satchel at her side, considerably lighter now that it's been relieved of all her books.

Good thinking.

Let's just hope we find her soon.

I have no doubt Maeve has Natasha. The girl I know wouldn't have gone willingly.

Whatever she's up to, it isn't by choice.

Natasha's path takes us on a winding route, which eventually leads back to the river. But this time it's deeper in the jungle. The trees are older and taller, and sunlight occasionally lances down through a break in the canopy. Everywhere we look is a riot of color and life. It's exquisite, and to some (like Sebastian and his sister) a little terrifying too. There are creatures here even more dangerous than the snakes—we must be on our guard at all times.

We stop for a moment at the river's edge to top off our canteens. But before we can drink from them, Kalia cries out.

"Wait!"

We all pause, surprised.

"Natasha filled the canteens right before we fell asleep. She must've done something to them."

"It *was* strange we all fell asleep so suddenly when we only meant to stop for lunch." Jemma says.

"Maeve was controlling her even then," Kalia says, her hands squeezing into fists. Then she dumps the remains of her water on the riverbank. The rest of us follow suit and rinse our canteens thoroughly in the rushing water before refilling them again. The river is much wider here, and the water looks deeper too. All sorts of new plant life grows on the banks, full of color and life.

We've hardly started on our way again before a scream pierces through the maze of vines and leaves.

Natasha.

Renewed urgency fills our limbs. Despite our exhaustion, we break into a run in the direction of the screams. They continue, but are strangely muffled. I hope one of those snakes hasn't gotten her—or worse.

I reach out with my magic. This time, I find Maeve's body walking talent easily—I'd recognize that sickly feeling anywhere—but the mind inside is frustrated. I catch a glint of Natasha, her terror bringing her own mind closer to the surface for a moment, but not enough to fight off the magic Maeve wields over her.

I have no idea what's going on. I just know it isn't good.

When we reach the source of the screams, we skid to a stop, gasping. Not far from the bank of the river is the most bizarre plant I've ever seen. It's enormous—the size of a carriage—with a thick green base and odd bright-blue appendages. Each one has two sides shaped like half-moons with white fronds on the ends, almost like the many legs of a centipede.

One of them is clamped shut. And moving. A lot. The muffled screams come from inside it.

"It has Natasha!" Sebastian cries.

"What *is* that thing?" Kalia says.

Rachel takes a step backward, drawing us with her. "I've heard of them, but never seen one before. Carnivorous plants. They eat animals to survive."

"We can't let it eat Natasha!" I cry. I try to latch on to some sort of mind inside the plant. But there are no thoughts, no consciousness to find. However it caught Natasha, it must be an automatic, instinctual reaction.

But we still need to get her out of there.

Kalia pushes past Rachel and grabs the nearest fallen branch. She pounds on the outside of the lobes trapping Natasha and yells at the top of her lungs, all while dodging the two other lobes that lunge for her.

Rachel and I follow suit, and before Jemma can stop him,

so does Sebastian. It's a terrifying plant, but we can't just sit back and let it devour our friend. Within a few minutes, the plant loosens its grip, and Natasha tumbles out onto the jungle floor, still clutching her pack. She scrambles away from the plant as fast as she can. The plant finally stops moving altogether, placing its appendages out in such a way that they look almost like leaves. That must be how Natasha was caught; it seemed strange, but harmless. Until it wasn't.

Natasha gets to her feet with fire in her eyes. My talent quickly confirms the worst.

"Maeve still has her," I say.

Rachel frowns and rummages through her bag.

"Simone, you should come with me. You belong with your mother." The words are Maeve's, but they come from Natasha's mouth and sound like her voice. I shudder. It is terrible to watch my friend be reduced to my mother's puppet.

Jemma approaches Natasha with her hands out in a calming gesture. "Look, just give us back what you stole, all right?"

Natasha laughs. "I don't think so. I appreciate the rescue, but I'm leaving—"

Rachel, who was circling, comes up behind her and threads

an obsidian pendant around her neck, severing Maeve's connection. Natasha's words choke off, and she blinks rapidly before bursting into tears. She falls to her knees, and Sebastian, Kalia, and I rush forward to throw our arms around her.

We know what it feels like. The awful sense of being a stranger in your own body. To have someone else moving your lips and saying words you'd never think to utter.

We've got you now, I tell her mind to mind. *You're safe.*

When she stops crying, we help her to her feet, and she wipes her eyes. Then she shoves her pack at Rachel. "Please take them. Before she tries to use me again."

Rachel removes her books, then hands it back. "It's all right. We know it wasn't really you. Maeve is devious."

"And always looking for any opportunity, it seems," Jemma says.

I take Natasha's hand and squeeze it. "Keep that obsidian necklace on this time. Did you lose your amulet?"

She nods. "It must have caught on something while we fled the villagers. I had no idea until it was too late."

"Do you need to rest for a few minutes before we press on?" Rachel asks.

Natasha stands up straighter, her mouth forming a hard line. "No. I'm all right. Just a bit shaken, but that will pass." She glances back at the carnivorous plant. "I'd like to get out of the jungle sooner rather than later."

"Me too," Sebastian agrees.

"Then let's get moving," Jemma says.

After consulting Rachel's map, we locate the fastest route out of the jungle that will keep us heading in the right general direction. The chase took us through most of the jungle, and if we follow the river, we should reach the plains by nightfall.

I walk quickly alongside my companions, lost in my head, brushing over the fish in the river and their slippery thoughts in order to give my friends their privacy.

If I can do better about controlling my own talent, maybe then I can convince Maeve to be better too.

CHAPTER EIGHT

We cleared the jungle last night and part of me misses it. Fascinating creatures and flowers filled it though it was quite noisy. But animal thoughts are different from people thoughts. They're more about emotions and colors and images than distracting words. It isn't quite so dizzying. While the others were scared by some of the animals, I didn't mind the snakes so much once I convinced them to release us. Their scales were lovely, and really they were only hungry. I can't blame them for that.

It was nice to spend time with creatures who aren't mad at me, or thinking of me as foolish. I'm weary of those constant thoughts from my companions. The simple desire for food and kinship is much easier to bear.

But we left it behind and this morning we make our way toward the seacoast. That's where we expect to pick up Maeve's trail again.

When we stop for lunch, Rachel sits next to Jemma and pulls out one of her books to read. I recognize its pale-green cover. She's been poring over this one for the last two days.

I turn my attention to other things, like feeding bits of bread to some inquisitive birds, but soon I notice that Rachel's face grows paler and paler with every moment.

It can't be…can it? Could they really…

"Could they what?"

She startles and gives me a look that tells me I'm not welcome in her thoughts. But then her expression softens. "I…I think we might be on the wrong path."

This gets the others' attention.

"What?" Jemma says, glancing over Rachel's shoulder.

Rachel frowns as the rest of our party gathers around us. "I don't know for sure, but this town record has a different account of where the soul summoner went."

"What town?" Jemma asks.

"Folton, which now lies near Lake Uccello. Only it didn't at the time this was written."

A strange sensation swims through my gut. Lake Uccello is the body of water that buried my lost hometown, Wren, after Lady Aisling stole all the talented people there a long time ago. The soul summoner lived there once too.

"Well, what does it say?" Natasha asks.

"It starts out the same in that Lake Uccello appeared overnight, the work of a grieving water wisher whose loss was so great she couldn't stop crying. They say she drowned the entire village of Wren and the surrounding area in her tears." Rachel clears her throat. "But then instead of leaving everything behind and departing the three territories to ensure they were safely out of the villain's reach, it says that the land she stood upon became an island, one that is permanently shrouded in fog. The remaining survivors of Wren were with her, and they've been hidden away there ever since."

A shocked silence descends on us all, only broken by Rachel clearing her throat again.

"I've read this passage four times and it all bears out with the facts we know. Lake Uccello is a saltwater lake, something that has always been surprising, because it's nowhere near the ocean or salt mines. The lake is well known for its constant fog too. All the tales talk of a lost island, but this account is the only one we've found from that time period, and it puts the island in a very different location. Here in the three territories." She looks around, wide-eyed. "I think that's where we'll find the soul summoner, if they're still alive as Devynne suggested and Maeve seems to believe. And if not, perhaps we'll just find their tomb and that will be the end of that."

"You mean... Wren might still be there on an island?" Ever since I discovered that my home had been replaced by a lake, I'd assumed all hope was lost. But this tale Rachel found... It sounds as though part of my village might live on. All they'd need is a life bringer and youth keeper to keep them alive.

Jemma smiles at me. "Yes, Simone. I think we may finally find your home after all."

Strange emotions roil inside me, and I don't know how to reconcile them. I'm too afraid to hope. But this threatens that resolve. My hands quiver, and I tuck them inside my cloak. When I look up, Sebastian smiles at me warmly, but I quickly glance away with a lump in my throat. Still, I can't help hearing his thoughts.

What exciting news! To think, they've been hiding there all along...

"How do we get there from here?" Jemma asks.

"Let's see." Rachel pulls out the map and considers it. "Well, if we keep going toward the ocean, we can take a boat down the coast and bypass the jungle and most of the mountains if we get out here at this port." She points to a village that's bordered by the ocean on one side and tall red cliffs that lead to a broad expanse of plains on the other. "Then we can make better time and get to Lake Uccello. That should be faster than braving the jungle again."

I only hope Maeve hasn't already gotten there first. If she figured this out before we did, all hope is lost.

I pat Rachel's arm encouragingly. She looks up in surprise, but this time she doesn't admonish me for reading her mind.

"Then let's go see the ocean," Natasha says, grinning. *I've always wanted to see it*, she thinks.

So have I. It sounds enormous and daunting and beautiful all at once.

We pack up our lunch and return to the road. Soon the grass under our feet is replaced by sand and the trees by small shrubs and the occasional flower.

Then, midafternoon, I finally see it. The ocean. The sandy beach churns under our feet, and water stretches out in front of us endlessly. Frothy waves crash onto rocks and sand like angry fists, then slip away again like an inhaled breath. The color is a deep greenish-blue, and the noise coming from it is strange. Thunderous, but with an undercurrent of a hundred whispers all speaking at once. I don't know what lives in the ocean, but I can't deny I'm rather curious to find out.

My feet take me closer until the sand becomes more solid. I remove my shoes and let it squelch between my toes. I laugh and twirl as a wave tickles my feet. Everything smells of brine and fresh air. The wind whips over my body and hair, tugging them behind me like a kite. I savor the moment, sure Jemma or Rachel will check me any second. But then Sebastian joins me, and Kalia and Natasha too. Jemma and Rachel aren't far behind, and we all splash and laugh in the ocean spray. For a few minutes we're free of our mission, our grave task, and just enjoy the sweetness of the life we wish for.

But soon we return to the beach. We take a few minutes to sit and watch the waves play while we rest our feet. When we finally head for the village in the distance, our minds and bodies feel renewed and hopeful.

We've discovered something that Maeve may not know. We might be able to beat her after all.

Last night, after we found a place to stay, Jemma secured us passage on a boat. This morning, we prepare to board—the first time on a ship for most of us. We're still wary of the inn and tavern staff, but we're hopeful that we might finally be a step ahead of Maeve.

I have no memories of being on a boat before, and neither does Sebastian. Kalia, though, loves them.

"I grew up by the sea," she tells us with a grin. "Family of fishers. We practically lived on boats. Careful, though. It can be rough on people who aren't used to it."

Natasha rubs her arms as we walk up the ramp onto the ship. "I've never been on one. Never even seen one before."

"Me neither," Sebastian agrees, eyes wide, as if that will help him take it all in faster.

I'm charmed and fascinated. The boat seems to roll under our feet, making it tricky to walk and stay upright at the same time. Gulls line the railing and hop across the deck, only to be shooed away by the sailors. The friendly waves crash against the sides, while the sailors hoist the rigging and ready the sails for departure. The wind whips through my hair, sending it every which way, and I brush the white strands back even though it's a futile effort. It's sunny and lovely and warm, and I wish to stay on deck investigating every odd new thing.

But we have other plans.

Before I can wander far, Rachel guides me belowdecks along with the rest of our group. We settle into a cabin, and Rachel takes out the map again, spreading it before us on a small table.

"All right. We're headed here." She uses her talent to make a small x on the map near Lake Uccello. "We know Maeve is either on the route we *were* on, but farther ahead, or if she also learned about the island in the middle of Lake Uccello, then she is probably on her way there. Or perhaps she's on another route entirely. She has the soul summoner's journal, after all, and we have no idea what clues that might contain." Several more lines appear on the map as Rachel marks those too. "Which means she is either already at her destination and we're way too late—"

"That seems unlikely," I interrupt. "If she had what she wanted, I'd know. The only thing left would be to come for me."

Rachel clears her throat, uncomfortably. "True. Which means she may have had a few false leads to follow first. And that we might be able to lie in wait for her, here." She marks another spot on the map on the way to the lake at the place where our paths should converge.

"What exactly are we going to do when she gets there?" Sebastian asks, wrinkling his nose. I'm wondering the same thing.

"Delay her. Distract her. Anything to keep her from getting to the island," Natasha says, suddenly full of determination. "I can do it. We'll find where we need to go, then I'll create illusions to lead her astray. We can send her right into a trap and keep her there while we go warn the people on the island that they're not safe."

My heart begins to race in my chest. That might work.

Natasha's illusion craft is impeccable. It's impossible to tell the difference between an illusion and the real thing unless you try to touch one and only get air. I don't know how long Maeve would be fooled but hopefully long enough to give us time to get to the island first.

Or lead her into a trap as Natasha suggests.

"What kind of a trap?" Kalia asks.

"Maybe a pit? Or a cage of some sort?" Natasha sits up straighter. "We can enlist the help of guards from Folton, that other local village, perhaps. We can trick her into falling into a pit, and they'll keep her there under guard until we get back."

"We'd have to be sure they all wore obsidian," Jemma mused. "But yes, that might work."

"You're forgetting something," I say suddenly. "Melanthe."

Everyone immediately sobers. Our friend, the mind mover, is a dangerous foe. And she's currently under Maeve's control.

"She could toss aside the guards like dolls if Maeve wanted her to," Sebastian says. "And then lift Maeve out of a pit with her mind alone."

"Any plan we make must be sure to take her out of the picture first," Rachel says. "Can we use your illusion, Natasha, to separate her from Maeve without either of them realizing it? Then we can get some obsidian around her neck to free her."

Natasha considers. "Possibly. It will all depend on the place where we decide to make our stand. The landscape and layout will determine a lot."

Rachel nods. "Then we'll plan for what we can now, but with some flexibility until we get to our destination."

Kalia frowns. "We'll have to be careful though. Maeve also has Elias. It will be easy to get confused if she's using him too."

Elias is a thought thrower, and deceptively powerful. He can put thoughts in your head so convincingly that you can hardly distinguish them from your own. He's manipulated more than one person into doing things they might not otherwise with his magic. Maeve could easily lead us astray with his talent if she wanted to.

The others keep chattering, their mouths and minds a loud blur that makes me dizzy. I focus as best I can, but finally pick up one of Rachel's books to look through. I do my best to get lost in the pages, while the others finesse our plan to put an end to my mother's wickedness.

Maybe I'm just tired. Or weak with caring for her. But

I can't bring myself to excitedly plan her destruction like my friends are doing.

I have my own plan anyway.

The next time we encounter Maeve, I'll find a way to reason with her. To make her see that what she's doing is wrong.

It may be my one and only chance to save her.

CHAPTER NINE

We spend most of the day and one night at sea. Natasha has decided boats are definitely not for her, but Sebastian and I love them. After the planning session yesterday, we went back up to the deck and watched the beach and docks disappear until all we could see in every direction was water. It felt peaceful, like we were alone in the world on that ship, the last of everything.

But this morning land came into sight. We leaned over the railing, craning our necks. These beaches have ruddy-colored sand, unlike the white sand of the first beach we saw. The shoreline is framed by tall red cliffs that seem to shoot straight up into the sky, topped by plains and beyond the beginnings of a forest.

According to Rachel's map, if we make our way around the cliffs, we can march straight through the forest until we reach Lake Uccello.

The closer we get to our destination, the more nervous I become. My stomach feels permanently tied up in knots. Wren, a place I've longed to find, might still exist on a secret island in the fog-shrouded lake. I'd all but given up hope. I don't know what to do now that it's been unexpectedly rekindled.

Moving forward is, I suppose, the only answer.

Soon the boat moors at the dock and we disembark, Kalia the most wistfully.

I'll be glad when this is over and I can go home again. I hate leaving the ocean...

Her pain comes through clearly even though I wasn't trying to dip into her thoughts. This must end. Maeve must be stopped.

My hands ball into fists at my sides. I know what I have to do. I wish it didn't scare me so.

But I must, for my friends and my newfound family. Too much hangs in the balance.

The gulls dive and swoop, and I let my senses devour the

smell of the seashore one more time before we head for the village proper. It is quaint, all seaside cottages with shells for shingles and white stucco sides. Driftwood and seashells decorate the yards, along with a few scattered rosebushes and patches of long grasses.

A few other travelers were on the ship, too, and together we make our way to the inn in the center of town. But the locals are not quite as welcoming as some of the people in other places we've been. Faces peer out from the windows we pass, appraising us without a greeting.

Curious, I send my talent spinning out.

Who are they…

Are they with her?

I hope they don't have talents…

I shudder. "Maeve must've already been here," I whisper to my friends. "I don't think she made a good impression."

Jemma frowns. "Can you tell what she did?"

I shake my head. "No one is thinking of a specific incident. But several seem to be afraid of the comet-blessed."

"Then we need to be careful," Natasha says, rubbing her arms.

"Let's not use our talents while we're here, all right?" Rachel says. "Just to be safe."

We all agree, but I worry about keeping that promise. Half the time I don't even mean to use my talent; it just happens.

"We won't stay long, though, will we?" asks Sebastian.

"Just for breakfast. Then we'll be on our way," Jemma says.

Sebastian nods at me encouragingly. He knows what a challenge this will be for me. I turn my head away, keeping my talent close and my mind closed.

We reach the tavern, but it's quieter than we expected. The other travelers with us seem confused, but take it in stride.

A man stands behind the bar in the center of the tavern. "Hello there," he says, with a smile that doesn't quite reach his eyes. "What can I get you?"

An older couple who also came off the boat speak up first. "Just looking for a bite to eat, and a place to stay for a night." The older man leans back and smiles at his wife. "We're visiting relatives in the town of Celdano, but we're in no hurry to get there."

His wife laughs. "They're not our favorite relatives, you see. But they are the richest, so we must pay our respects every so often."

The tavern keeper nods, then takes their order. "And where are you young folks traveling?" he asks.

Rachel speaks first. "Jemma and I are the children's governesses. We've been on holiday just up the coast, but now we're meeting their parents in Folton."

He gives each of us the once-over.

That other woman was traveling with strange children too. I wonder if they're connected somehow...

I step forward, hoping to interrupt his train of thought. "We're mighty hungry. Any hope of griddle cakes?"

Jemma gives a strained laugh as she puts a hand on my shoulder. "Don't mind Simone. She's always like this in the morning until there's food in her belly."

The tavern keeper nods. "Then we best take care of that."

We place our order, and his mind only touches on Maeve once or twice more. We find a table in the corner by a window and wait for our meals. We aren't the only ones who came here for breakfast. While we wait, several more people arrive. Villagers, if their friendliness with the tavern keeper is any indication. And the suspicious looks they give us and every other stranger in the room.

When our food arrives, we waste no time tucking in, though every one of us has nerves strung tight as a bowstring. We must eat quickly before the villagers discover our connection to Maeve.

I am almost finished with my griddle cakes when a hush suddenly falls over the room. A large man stands in the middle of the tavern, staring straight at us.

Beside me, Sebastian nearly chokes on his bite of egg. The other two men at the table stand too. My entire body quivers as I reach into their minds—and find Maeve.

Come with me, she whispers, *and there won't be any trouble.*

I murmur to Rachel, eyes wide. "It's Maeve. She's here for me."

Rachel's arm tightens around me. "She won't have you." She turns to the others at our table. "Quickly, quietly, leave now."

We slide out of our table as fast as we can, but the men march toward us. The other villagers rise from their chairs, some of them trying to hold back the men.

Jemma grabs me by hand and drags me out the door, just before the largest man lunges for me. The villagers slam the tavern door closed and do their best to delay and restrain my would-be captors.

We don't dare to waste this reprieve. We run straight out of town and into the wooded hills beyond.

CHAPTER TEN

Now that we've finally entered the forest and are on our way to Lake Uccello, it should be a relief. But I'm not comforted, or even excited as I thought I'd be. Instead, I feel strange. Everything feels odd and out of place. I have no idea what we'll find at the island, assuming it really exists and I haven't just gotten my hopes up again for nothing.

Not to mention, I'm terrified at the prospect of seeing my mother again.

She's taking people over indiscriminately now, willing to use anyone and anything that might serve her cause. I feel terrible—guilty even—that we didn't have time to give those poor people in that last village obsidian to protect them.

It makes it even more difficult than usual to concentrate on the path we should be taking. My feet have their own ideas, and more than once, Kalia, Natasha, or Sebastian gently nudges me back in the right direction.

I'd be lost without them. But it feels like I have to make a choice: them or Maeve. I don't know how to choose between my real family and my found one.

When night falls, we make camp. According to Rachel's map, we should reach the lake in a day and a half at most. My insides feel all fizzy and weak at the thought of it. But the others are excited.

"If this works, we could be on our way home soon," Kalia says. Her thoughts are buoyant, and if I wasn't so nervous, they'd be infectious.

Natasha grins at her. "That would be wonderful."

Sebastian steals a glance at me. "It would be nice to go back home," he says. "It feels like I haven't been there in forever."

Jemma gives his arm a squeeze.

You'll come home with us, right? Sebastian thinks at me. But I don't answer. I honestly don't know. Ever since we were released from Lady Aisling's control, I've known someday I'd need to go and find my real home. But then I discovered Wren disappeared, its villagers gone without much of a trace. And now, it turns out, it might still exist.

I have no idea what I want, let alone what I'm going to do.

So I don't answer. Instead, I look away and focus on chewing my dinner.

The more I retreat, the more worried Sebastian gets. But I don't know how to talk to him anymore. Every time I try to speak with him, my tongue feels tied up in knots. I have no words of comfort to offer, not like I used to.

So I avoid him and his mind instead and lay out my bedroll before everyone else. The embers of the fire dance and make shadows play on the insides of my eyelids while I try to rest.

Though my friends have all fallen asleep, my anxious mind refuses to release me to slumber. Every shadow is a mirage, even though I know Natasha's talent isn't on the loose. Even the chittering animals in the trees are no comfort tonight, only a further distraction. I pull my talent close. I don't want it to wander. But the stars shine overhead and the moon seems to loom closer than ever. I turn on my side, squeezing my eyes shut.

That's when I hear it. It begins as a rustling—not an unusual thing for the forest at night—somewhere off in the bushes between the trees. I ignore it at first. We're in the woods. I know full well there are strange sounds aplenty here. They've never scared me before. Then the sound gets louder and a branch snaps as though something heavy has stepped on it. Like a foot.

I open my eyes and sit bolt upright. Dark shadowed figures circle the camp. We're surrounded.

Maeve has found us at last.

My body rises off the ground. I scramble for my pack, determined to at least keep something close.

Melanthe's talent must be behind this.

"Help!" I cry, but only a little sound comes out. My cloak covers my mouth, held there by Melanthe's magic to muffle any screams I might make.

I send my talent wide until I light upon several minds, more than I thought Maeve had with her. My heart drops into my feet like an anchor.

She's collecting talented folks to use.

I shudder. In her desperation to fulfill her quest, Maeve is becoming everything she hates. She's so blinded by her grief she can't see it. I must get through to her somehow. Make her see that what she's doing is wrong.

That's when I make my decision. Her minions are only after me. If I don't wake my friends, it will stay that way. If I do, she'll be forced to fight to steal me away. That won't end well. I can't risk my friends.

I'll go with Maeve willingly. It's the only way I have a chance of convincing her to set aside her terrible plan and free these poor people she's enslaved. I'm her daughter; I'm the only one who could make her see the light.

If I can't do it, no one can.

But for now, I focus on Melanthe. Her mind is lost and desperate inside her helpless body. *I'm sorry, I'm sorry, I'm sorry* runs on repeat, and it brings tears to my eyes.

Maeve has used Melanthe's talent to pluck me from the safety of my friends and into the woods where she waits. It's a strange feeling having my friend's talent used on me. I float through the air, but an odd tug pulls me forward like an invisible, giant hand.

There's no sense in struggling. I already know that. The only hope I have of breaking free is reaching Melanthe's mind beneath Maeve's dominant one. But can I even do that? Could I help her overthrow Maeve, even without obsidian? I have no idea, but it won't hurt to try. Especially if my plan to sway my mother back toward good fails.

The trees march by as the invisible hand weaves my body between them toward wherever Maeve hides. I concentrate as hard as I can, probing deeper into Melanthe's mind. She feels so far away, but I search and search and delve further than I ever have before. I call out to her, mind to mind, hoping for a response. But all I get is that same faint refrain of *I'm sorry*. She's deeply buried under Maeve's power.

And Maeve's talent is *strong*.

Suffocatingly so. She hasn't noticed me digging around yet, but she might soon. The deeper I dig, the more the weight of her magic presses down on me. Finally I yank my talent back, gasping and exhausted.

But Melanthe's constant stream of I'm-sorrys felt closer and louder than they did at first. Maybe if I keep at it, practice at little more, I'll actually be able to help someone under Maeve's thumb.

The moon shines high above, brilliantly lighting up the grove where Maeve waits. Melanthe finally sets me down before my mother.

"Simone," Maeve says, wrapping me in an embrace. I couldn't hug her back, even if I wanted to. Melanthe still holds me tight in case I try to run. "How I've missed you. Finally, you're back where you're supposed to be. With your mother."

"You stole me from my friends." I frown. "How did you even find us?" We've been very careful about not telling anyone our plans.

Maeve just smiles. "I have my ways. Besides, I knew you'd come this way. After you got on that boat, this was the most likely route to Lake Uccello. I've been waiting for you."

Shock hits me like a bucket of ice water. "This was all a trap."

Maeve shrugs. "I did what any mother would to recover her lost child."

"But how?"

She raises an eyebrow at me. "I have the soul summoner's journal. I learned about the island in the lake weeks ago. I knew it wouldn't be long before you figured it out. So I've been traveling, gathering help while I waited for you. After all, we're a family. And families help each other." Her eyes bore into me. "I will need your help to get to the soul summoner."

If Melanthe wasn't holding me fast with her magic, I'd take a step back. As it is, I'm stuck in Maeve's embrace. Terror burns in my chest, spreading outward through my limbs.

I was waiting for this, knew at some point she'd come for me. But I wasn't expecting was how terrified I'd be once she had me. Maeve has changed since I last saw her. Gone is the kind, strong woman I loved. In her place is a stranger driven mad by grief. Her mind is a wreck. She can still keep me out of places she doesn't wish me to wander, but the pristine order is in more disarray, though her focus is now clear and so sharp it cuts. The hunt for her family, and the soul summoner who can bring them back, consumes her.

For the first time, I begin to doubt whether I can change her mind.

My voice shakes when I speak. "What of my friends? They will come for me once they realize what you've done."

"It doesn't matter. We'll be too far on our way to our destination when they wake up." Maeve leans down and cups my face in her hands, beaming at me. "We're going home at last."

CHAPTER ELEVEN

We slip away under the cover of darkness, leaving my friends far behind. The lake should be a little over a day of travel away, but I don't know what other talents Maeve has under her control. She could have one that will speed up the pace. It would explain why she's so confident.

I suppose that's what happens—when you have too much power, you begin to believe nothing can stop you or stand in your way for long.

For my part, I'm exhausted and soon find myself tripping along behind my mother. She stops after the third time I stumble over a fallen branch or root or rock.

"My dear, how silly of me. You must be so tired. Don't

worry. I'll carry you," Maeve says. Then Melanthe raises her arms. Suddenly, my feet no longer touch the ground. The others begin to march again, and I'm whisked along by the strength of Melanthe's mind and the force of my mother's magic.

Though my eyes beg to close and sleep as I'm carried, I study the others who accompany us. I assume they're all talented, though it's possible she picked up others who just happened to be useful for one reason or another.

My talent brushes over their minds. Some I recognize, like Elias and Melanthe. Others I'm not familiar with. I try prying into their heads but Maeve holds the reins tightly, and I'm too exhausted to dig further.

Tomorrow will be a different story.

I finally give myself over to sleep, saying a silent prayer that my friends rise early and come to rescue me.

When I wake, the sun is high enough in the sky to tell me that it's midmorning. Almost by instinct I reach out with my magic to find Sebastian, or any of my other friends.

I don't feel them anywhere nearby. Wherever they are, they're too far away for me to detect.

Heat begins to burn behind my eyes. What if I can't persuade Maeve? What if I fail and the soul summoner is used to bring back her family, and then the gift giver is forced to return Lady Aisling's talent? The enormity of it feels like a rock pressing on my chest and makes it hard to breathe.

"Are you awake now, little one?" Maeve says when we stop for breakfast. I don't know how Maeve was able to march all night without sleep. Perhaps she's been sleeping during the day, or she has a talent to help her.

"Yes," I say. "I can walk on my own now."

Maeve raises an eyebrow. "Can I trust you? Or do you plan to run again?"

"I won't run. I…I need to talk to you. It's very important."

"Then come here and let's talk." She pats the log she sits on and I join her. She hands me an apple from her bag, along with what smells like a fresh roll. I tear into them both.

"How many people do you have with you now?" I ask, gesturing to the others who stand like silent sentinels in a ring around the clearing where we eat. "Don't they need to eat too?"

She shrugs. "They eat twice a day. It's enough to keep them going." She chews on a roll of her own. "I have many helpers now. I haven't bothered to count. But everywhere I go, every village I visit, I acquire more people who can help me in my mission. We're like a family of our own in some ways." She smiles, but it feels strange and distorted, not warm and kind like it used to.

I glance at the sentinels warily. There are people of all ages guarding us. I wonder how many are missing their homes and families. Forced to go along with Maeve's terrible plot.

"What do they do? Why are they so useful to you?"

She laughs. "You'll find out."

I frown. "I don't understand how you can take these people from their homes and use them like this. It's what Lady Aisling did to you, to me." Tears begin to fall, sopping my cheeks.

Maeve wipes my tears away with her thumb. "I'm not holding them prisoner. We're out seeing the world! And we're working toward a noble cause." She harrumphs. "Lady Aisling kept us prisoner for her own selfish, greedy ends. As playthings. An amusement. Parlor tricks at her lavish parties." She shook her head. "No, what I'm doing is completely different."

My heart begins to pound. I knew this wouldn't be easy. But I didn't count on it being this hard either.

"It may be different to you, but what about for them? They're being forced to do things for you. Against their will."

She narrows her eyes at me. "What are you implying?"

I swallow hard. Suddenly I feel very small indeed. "Just that…to some, your way of going about your mission might seem just as selfish as what Lady Aisling did."

Maeve's face begins to flame and her mouth hardens into a straight line. "You're calling your own mother, who only wants to reunite our family, selfish?" She shakes her head as if she can't believe what I said. Her tone is worse than any slap would be.

"I worry she's influenced you so much that you can't see straight. I know you grieve our family. I do too." I put my hand on her arm tentatively. "But I think it's blinding you to the truth."

She glances at me with fire in her eyes. "Simone, I will only say this once. I'm nothing like the Lady. I don't want to hear those words out of your mouth ever again. These people are helping us. And you will help me, too, whether you like it or not."

I suck my breath in sharply. "What do you mean?"

"You will be my eyes and ears on this mission. And if you refuse, I will make you do it anyway." With that, she stalks off to put away the remains of our breakfast.

Horror courses through me. She wouldn't. She *couldn't* do that to me. Her daughter.

Would she?

My hands quiver and I shove them in my pockets.

The truth is, I don't know. I didn't believe she would before. But now...I'm no longer so certain. She's absolutely determined to do whatever it takes to reach her goal, even more so than the last time I spoke to her. Then, she promised me something I've cherished as truth: that if there was a way to bring our family back without harming my friends or anyone else, she'd do it.

It seems like she may have already forgotten.

CHAPTER TWELVE

Maeve's minions trail after us like ribbons in the wind. Their faces are blank, expressionless. All of them walk in perfect unison. Maeve's in their heads, pulling their strings and keeping their own minds down. I shiver.

When I was being controlled, my mind was so damaged that I could hardly speak as I normally would. I retreated into my thoughts, and half of anything that came from my mouth was strange or unintelligible.

I hope these other talented folks Maeve has stolen do not become as damaged as we were. I hope they can find peace eventually.

I must find a way to free them. I wish I'd had time to grab some of those obsidians out of Rachel's bag before Melanthe stole me from the camp. Maeve knows we've somehow cut off her talent before, but I don't think she suspects what it was. Yet. I've kept my necklace carefully hidden under my dress.

But maybe there's another way. I made an attempt last night to reach down and pull up Melanthe. I got close to finding her in there, but was too exhausted to go any further. Now, I've made up my mind that as long I'm in control of my own talent, I will keep trying to reach one of them.

Maeve hasn't tied me up, but I'm surrounded by her captives. She knows I can't go far without her easily recapturing me. And she knows I know it too. That much is clear from her thoughts. She hasn't spoken to me since I accused her of being like Lady Aisling.

The sun is clear and high over our heads, rising with every step we take. The trees spread their green leaves wide, basking in the warmth and light. It's very hot today, even in the shade of the forest. And humid too. The air feels as thick as porridge. It makes it hard to breathe, but that doesn't slow Maeve in the slightest.

I empty my water canteen quickly. Soon I'm terribly thirsty.

"Maeve? Can we find a place for more water?" She doesn't even turn around, but one of her minions breaks ranks and snatches my canteen from me. She's an older woman, with graying hair but bright, clear eyes. Without missing a step, she mumbles quietly and seconds later water sloshes inside the canteen again. She hands it back wordlessly and returns to her position.

A water wisher. Maeve is collecting people she finds useful.

"Thank you," I say to both of them.

Maeve's focus is razor sharp, and she ignores me, even though her thoughts reveal she's glad to have me nearby again.

I am going to do one thing on this journey: focus my own talent to try to pry loose Maeve's grip on these people. Since I worked with Melanthe last night, I decide to start with the water wisher today.

Crossing my fingers, I set my talent loose on the older woman. I've searched Maeve's mind for the names of her new captives, but it seems she never bothered to learn all of them before stealing them away.

It must be easier to do what she's doing if she doesn't know much about them. They're faceless to her. Just talents for her to use. I shudder. She's becoming so much like the Lady that it's getting harder and harder to see the differences.

The water wisher's mind is well hidden, but the deeper I pry, the louder her pleas for help become. She's confused and doesn't seem to understand what's happening. I must be very careful.

I need to know if I can do this. So I keep working on the water wisher. Her mind is shoved so far down it feels impossible to reach her. But little by little, my magic peels away the layers Maeve's talent has laid down. Then I try talking to her, just her, so that Maeve can't hear even though her mind is in control.

Hello, I'm a mind reader. I want to help you. Can you hear me?

The first few times I attempt this, I receive no response. Her pleas for help continue. I keep going, though my efforts begin to impact me physically. The heat and humidity make it difficult to breathe, and now it feels as if a weight sits on my chest. I barely even notice when I trip over a root and go flying until pain shoots through me as I hit the ground.

"Oh!" Maeve cries, turning toward me. "Are you all right?"

I blink, dazed and breathless. The arm I landed on throbs. She helps me up and sets me down on a nearby log.

"Did you trip?"

"I think so." When she rubs my arm, I yelp. She rolls up my sleeve to find a long scrape. I must've landed on a branch or rock that scratched right through my clothes.

"Let's clean this up before we go any farther. Can't have that getting infected." She uses water from her canteen and the edge of my cloak to clean and dry the cut, then digs in her bag until she finds a bandage. I suppose a first aid kit is a must when you're out in the wilds traveling with people who don't have control over their own limbs. Soon I'm all patched up.

"Thank you," I say, and mean it. I've always had to rely on others to take care of me, to think of the important details like this. I suppose I'm better off with my mother than alone.

Maeve brushes my wispy hair back from my face with a kind look that's so much like the ones she gave me when I first knew her that my breath catches in my throat. I miss this Maeve. The one I could love and trust. The one who would never harm me, only protect me. Is this person still that Maeve? She must be in there somewhere, even if I have to reach as far down to find her as I do her victims.

"I'll always take care of you, Simone. It's what mothers

do." She extends a hand to help me up. I take it tentatively and she pulls me into a hug. "I've missed you. But please remember, everything I'm doing, I do for *us*. For our family." When she releases me, she regards me appraisingly. "Do you need to rest a bit? It's nearly dinnertime."

We sit on the log and share a meal of cheese and bread and some berries she collected on our journey this afternoon. Her captives form a protective circle around us, facing outward toward the woods. My talent brushes over them one by one, but all I sense on the surface is the sickly feeling of Maeve's talent in use. It's so unlike how her actual mind feels that it would be easy to think of them as two different people if I didn't know better. But I do.

"Where did you go, little one?" Maeve says, turning my chin to face her. I realize that she's been speaking to me while I was lost in my own world.

"Sorry. I'm tired."

Maeve nods. "It's a long journey. I'll have Melanthe carry you the rest of the way."

Heat flashes over me. "No, no, that won't be necessary." I didn't enjoy the sensation of being tugged along like that, floating over everything. It was very unsettling. "I'll make do."

She frowns. "Are you sure? Truly, it's no trouble at all."

Except it *is* for Melanthe. I could sense how tired she was after using her talent for so long last night, but Maeve didn't care. Not until I was safely away from my friends.

"No, really, I'll be fine."

Despite knowing how futile it is, I send my talent as far as I can in what I believe to be the direction of my friends' camp. But they're still too far away. My heart sinks. That doesn't bode well for me.

I'll try again later. I can't let hopelessness overwhelm me yet.

"Once we get to Lake Uccello, I'll be depending on you to help me navigate. The lake is covered by a thick fog…" As Maeve lays out her plan to get to the island, I nod along, pretending to be surprised at the right moments. I don't want her to know how much my friends have figured out. We're all heading in the same direction. I just hope they catch up in time.

CHAPTER THIRTEEN

We make it to the lake late in the evening. My first glimpse of my former home takes my breath away. It appears suddenly, looking for all the world as if some giant just dropped it here by accident. Mountains rise up on either side, and the lake stretches right up to the tree line. Here and there, ancient skeletal trunks poke out of the water. Dark waves lap at the banks, and the hovering fog gives the lake an otherworldly feel. I can barely see more than a few feet out onto the water, but I know from Rachel's map that the lake is vast.

It's beautiful and eerie, and the whole place feels just as mournful as the legend suggests.

I can definitely believe an island might be hiding some-where in all that fog.

Maeve, however, only sees frustration.

"We should've walked faster," she says, then sets her servants about setting up camp for us and starting a fire. "We'll have to wake early and row harder tomorrow. Between the darkness and that fog, it's just too dangerous to try at night." She folds her arms across her chest. "Besides, we want them to welcome us. They don't need to know why I'm really here until it's too late." A small smile flits over her face.

Hope ignites in me. Maybe this break for rest will give my friends the time they need to catch up and rescue me. Maybe I can warn the islanders of Maeve's plan before she captures the soul summoner. Maybe, maybe, maybe...

My head spins with possibilities. Once the fire is burning, we retire to our bedrolls, and I try again in earnest to reach Melanthe. This time, Maeve's control is looser, but she isn't asleep yet. I'm unable to throw off her talent, but I get a little closer than the last time.

That's progress, at least, and I'll take it.

The next morning, we eat a hurried breakfast, and Maeve has her minions pack everything up twice as fast as they set things out the night before. While she's fixated on that, I take a few moments to search for a sign of my friends. If they kept walking longer than we did, they might have closed the distance between us.

At first, I don't feel any familiar minds. A sense of desperation clings to me. Maeve has been completely unresponsive to my pleas for reason. I may need to get out of this situation sooner than I'd thought.

Then I sense it. The shape of Rachel's mind. It's so comforting and unexpected that tears form in the corner of my eyes.

Rachel! I call out to her.

Simone! Can you tell us where you are? she asks. I can sense her surprise.

Right now we're in a clearing near the lake. Maeve is determined to get to the island as soon as possible. If she has any idea you're following her, she'll take action. She has a lot more talented people under her control now too. I'm not sure what they all do yet.

We'll be on our guard. Don't worry, we'll find you.

While the thoughts she sends me sound brave, underneath I hear the concern she feels about whether they can succeed. We've all worried about that from the moment we set out from the Archives.

"Simone!" Maeve barks my name, and I whirl around. To all appearances it must've looked as if I were talking to the bushes for a few moments.

"Sorry, yes?" I say, scuffing my boot in the dirt.

"Come along. We must be going now." She holds her hand out for me as if she expects me to take it. I keep my hands clasped behind my back instead, but walk beside her.

Maeve leads us down to the water and a little cove where a boat waits for us tied to one of those skeletal trees sticking out of the water. It's not big enough to take everyone. A half dozen break off from the group and get in the boat, and Maeve and I board too. The rest of them, including Elias and the water wisher, stand on the shore, facing in all directions to keep watch.

She's leaving them there as a trap for anyone who might want to follow us. My heart sinks.

The others under her control pick up the oars and begin to row. The boat whispers across the glassy water, and we sail straight into the rolling white fog. One of Maeve's captives is a boy about Natasha's age, seventeen or so with dark hair and gray eyes. Another is young woman with freckled skin and red hair who looks frail enough that the wind alone could break her in half. But she rows as swiftly as the others and couldn't complain even if she wanted to. The last is an older boy who is as plain as can be, but has a kind sort of face. It's blank right now, thanks to Maeve.

My mother turns to me. "Simone, it's time for you to do your part. You're our navigator. Somewhere on this lake there are minds. Find them and guide us to them."

My stomach turns.

"I won't do it." I set my jaw, trying to look braver than I feel.

Maeve's eyebrows lift in surprise. "Oh, yes, you will. Willingly or not."

Shocks chills me. "You mean you'd…you'd…take me over? Just like you did to them?"

"I don't want to. But I will if I have to."

"But I'm your daughter." Suddenly, I feel very alone, and very, very small.

"Which is exactly why you should be helping me without so much resistance." Maeve narrows her eyes. "Now, tell me which way we need to go."

"I won't do it."

Maeve's face purples, and she grits her teeth. "I'll take no pleasure in forcing you."

My hands ball into fists in my skirt. "I won't. I can't let you do this."

Maeve takes a deep breath, releasing some of her anger. "You have no say in what I do, child. You should've listened to me." She reaches out, and even though I shrink back, there's nowhere to run on this boat. I squeeze my eyes shut, hoping the obsidian around my neck does its job well. Magic tingles across my skin, but my mind is still my own. I breathe out a sigh of relief.

My mother, however, sits next to me, stunned. "What are you doing? It can't be your talent, because this happened before with Sebastian, and just the other day when you somehow freed Natasha from my spell." She takes hold of my shoulders and examines me shrewdly. I'm too frightened to say a word.

Her eyes home in on the chain around my neck. Until recently, I've never been one to wear jewelry. "This is new…" she murmurs, then pulls the pendant up from under my dress. She gasps. "A talisman. So *this* is how you've been blocking my magic."

"It's just a trinket. Jemma made it for me." It's an outright lie, but Maeve can't know that for certain.

Still, she doesn't believe me. "I doubt that very much," she says, and then she yanks the obsidian—my only defense—from my neck.

"Now," she says. "Let's try this again. If you don't direct us willingly, I will force you. It's up to you."

I choke back a sob. I have no choice. Not really. My mother has stolen it from me. That's the worst part of all.

With tears in my eyes, I let my talent run through the fog, keeping above the water. Finally, I feel the vague shape of a mind, then another and another, then quite a few, due north.

With a heavy heart I point in their direction. "That way," I whisper.

Maeve's minions row, turning the boat to the right bearing. The thick fog shrouds us. All I can hear is the whisper of the paddles through the water and the hiss of the boat sliding across the glassy surface.

My insides roil. My own mother tried to use her talent on me to bend my will to her own. It was only a threat before, one I hadn't really thought she'd make good on.

So here I am, occasionally correcting our course based on the feeling of several minds in the middle of the lake.

How could my own mother threaten to do the one thing I fear the most?

I twist my cold hands in my cloak. Once we arrive, I'll need to warn the soul summoner and gift giver, even if it means suffering under Maeve's talent. I may have to brave my worst fear, but if it saves people, then it will be worth it. I hope.

CHAPTER FOURTEEN

We seem to glide for hours, and my mind begins to wander, skipping over the gentle waves the boat leaves in its wake.

Suddenly, my breath catches in my throat, and I unwittingly let out a small gasp. My talent is loose for me to guide the boat, but it also detected something familiar not far behind us.

My friends. They're on their way. I was afraid they might have been delayed by Maeve's minions, but it seems they managed to evade them. If they can help us, that would be extraordinary.

"What is it, Simone?" Maeve says, narrowing her eyes at me.

"Nothing," I say, giving her my best innocent look.

"I don't believe you." She sighs. "You noticed something, didn't you? With your talent? Is someone else out there on the lake?"

The blood drains from my face, but I shake my head. "Of course not," I squeak out.

"It's your friends, isn't it?" Maeve turns to the boy with dark hair and gray eyes, Dasco, who has been sitting on the bow of the boat, quiet as can be. He and Melanthe are the only servants not rowing at the moment. He rises to his feet and lifts his arms high, throwing his head back. The air begins to stir, and the sky darkens as clouds gather overhead.

"What are you doing?" I ask, but Maeve doesn't answer. She turns away, having set Dasco to do whatever it is she needs him for.

The wind whips my hair across my face as I prod Maeve's mind.

I don't think so, daughter.

No one has ever been able to thwart my talent like she can. She must've learned how when I was a child. It would've been necessary raising a mind reader, but now it's frustrating.

So instead, I dig into Dasco's mind despite the sickly

feeling of Maeve's magic controlling him. My stomach turns as I catch a snippet of his thoughts. *No, please, I don't want to hurt anyone...*

Then he's gone, driven farther down by Maeve's insistent power.

The water turns choppy and I gape at my mother. "You can't. Please, don't do this!"

She shrugs. "They knew the risks."

"But they're taking them for *me*!"

"Why should they? You're right where you belong. With your mother." She pats my knee, and I flinch.

Dasco is a storm brewer. Maeve is using his talent to drive away my friends.

I close my eyes and reach out to feel the shape of Sebastian's mind. *Go back!* I think-shout at him. *Turn around before it's too late! Maeve has a storm brewer and she's using him right now.*

We're trying, Sebastian thinks back, a sharp, fearful edge to his thoughts. *But the water's getting so rough. We hardly have control over the boat anymore.*

Hang on! I tell him. Maeve won't listen to me, but I have to try anyway.

"Don't do this," I beg her. "They're my friends." Tears brim in my eyes. What would I do without Sebastian? I don't even know if he can swim. I don't even know if *I* can swim for that matter.

"They brought this on themselves," she says.

I set my talent on Dasco, prying into his mind, but he is pushed down even deeper than Melanthe was. Maeve's grip on him is firm. But I try nonetheless. Finally, I glimpse his mind again; the confusion is palpable and painful.

What's happening to me? What's happening to me? is all he can think.

Melanthe turns her attention toward the storm, holding up her hands and concentrating. I don't know what Maeve could be having her do now, and I don't want to find out.

The storm begins to rage in earnest. Rain pours down, followed by hail. Dasco makes a shoving motion with his hands, and suddenly all the bad weather moves toward the section we've left in our wake—right where my friends' boat must be. The strange weather controlled by Dasco's talent forms a stormy column, churning and frothing the water. Another of Maeve's captives suddenly comes to attention and begins to whistle—a wind whistler. He makes a wind that pushes us toward the island in the center. The faster we move, the fainter Sebastian's thoughts get.

But what I hear leaves me trembling.

Simone, the boat can't take much more. I don't even know how to swim. There are no more words, just panic and terror and then…nothing. I have no idea what's happening to him and no way to find out. Soon, we're too far away for me to hear his or any of my friends' thoughts.

I can't stop shaking. A terrible emotion brews inside me. My mother finally notices my distress.

"Come here, Simone." She tries to put an arm around me, but I recoil. I want to cry, but no tears come. Shock has ceased all normal functions. Maeve pulls back. "Remember when I told you once before that I would fight for you? I meant it. And I don't care who I'm fighting. I'll do anything to keep my family together."

I finally find my voice, though it's as hollow as I feel. "Sebastian and Jemma are my family."

For a moment, Maeve looks hurt. But then she scoffs and turns away. "They were never your family. They took care of you, and I'm grateful to them for that. But nothing can rival the bond between mother and child. It's for the best that they're gone. Now there's nothing more to distract you from our real purpose."

Something inside me cracks. I double over, letting out a forlorn cry.

"What do you mean, gone?" I manage to whisper.

Maeve brushes my hair back from my face—a gesture I once loved—even though I flinch again. "My dear, no one could survive the gale Dasco brought down on them. Unless they can breathe underwater, I assume they're gone."

"You...killed them?"

She shrugs as if it is nothing at all.

The crack rips in two. Tears fall fast and furious, until I can hardly breathe. I can't quite wrap my head around what Maeve has done. It aches like a physical wound.

Sebastian can't be dead. All I want to do is apologize for my coldness to him lately. To tell him he was right. I failed. Maeve *is* too far gone to be reached. The talent taker is the only way to stop her for good.

I can't take navigating anymore. I can't even think straight. I curl up in the bottom of the boat and let tears flood me.

I don't know how long I doze, but Maeve and her servants manage to get us to the island without me. I wake when the boat stops. When I open my eyes, I'm surprised to see Natasha has joined us. That must have been what Melanthe was doing while Dasco sent the storm after our friends. Maeve saved the only one she deemed useful.

And now Natasha is under her control again. That's my fault. I didn't mean to let Maeve know about obsidian, but I'm not a very good liar. Grief wells up in me again, and I turn away from my friend to hold it back.

Instead, I focus on the island. Lake Uccello may be buried in fog, but the island itself is bright and sunny and lovely. A sharp contradiction to the storm we just weathered. The small beach where we came ashore is all pebbled sands, surrounded by an embankment dripping with greenery. Giant ferns and young trees sprout from the earth, and pretty flowering vines cling to the latter. Any other day, I'd be charmed by it.

But all I can think about is Sebastian. His last cries for help hit me again like a punch to the gut.

Maeve helps me onto land and assigns most of her servants to wait with the boat. Natasha and Melanthe come with us.

"Where are they?" Maeve asks me. It's useless to resist her. I reach out and find the islanders' minds, then point wordlessly in the right direction.

We step into the forest, and I leave behind all hope of escape.

CHAPTER FIFTEEN

There are many well-trod paths crisscrossing the island. It is larger than I expected, but not enough to roam as freely as I'd like if I lived here. It almost makes me feel claustrophobic.

It isn't long before we see signs of a village, and my breath catches in my throat.

This is what's left of Wren. My home. And Maeve's.

I've longed for home for so long that I don't know what to do now that I've found it. My hands knit in my cloak, and a strained laugh bursts from my mouth. This isn't the happy reunion I'd wished for.

I'm here to help my mother betray them.

All the hope I cherished of convincing Maeve to abandon this mission has been crushed during the journey here. My friends are gone. They can't help me now. It's just me against Maeve and the hapless people she has under her control. I'll have to find the courage to stand up to her, even if it means I pay the ultimate price and suffer the thing I fear most.

Maeve stops us suddenly while we're still in the woods, yanking me from my thoughts. At her command, Natasha weaves an illusion, making us appear to be a small family with matching golden hair and blue eyes. The better to conceal who we really are from the villagers just in case they recognize us as their long-lost neighbors.

Then my mother addresses me with a dangerous gleam in her eyes. "Now, Simone. I hope you haven't gotten any foolish ideas about warning the villagers."

Heat warms my cheeks and I glance away. Maeve tugs my chin back to face her.

"I will only tell you this once: if you dare to betray me, your remaining friends will suffer the consequences."

My heart stutters in my throat. "What do you mean?"

Maeve straightens up, smoothing her skirt. "I only need

one vessel for the daughter I wish to bring back. I don't need both Melanthe and Natasha. If you go against me, I might decide one of them is expendable."

Suddenly, I can't breathe. She's already killed Sebastian; if I warn the villagers, I'm not just risking my own freedom; I'm risking one of my few remaining friends' lives.

"Do you understand me?" she says, waiting for a response.

I swallow the sand coating my throat. "Yes. I understand."

"Good. Let's go."

We draw near to the village, and the shape of it becomes clearer. The houses are made from stonework, and each well-crafted roof includes a small chimney. A few puff little clouds of woodsmoke. What stands out most is how quiet the village is. No one stops us at the gate. In fact, we don't see anyone at all, though I can feel the presence of minds.

I concentrate. There are maybe two dozen people here. And they're definitely aware of our presence.

Who are they?

How did they get here?

What could they want?

"What are you hearing, Simone?" Maeve asks.

"They're curious. Some are nervous."

As they should be. But I don't say that to my mother.

"Then we must allay their fears." Maeve clears her throat. "Hello! We were on Lake Uccello, and we got caught in a storm. It drove us here."

No one replies, but their minds light up with curiosity, so bright I can almost see it. Maeve glances at me, and I nod encouragement, though it twists my stomach to do so.

"The storm damaged our boat. My name is Maeve, and these are my children. May we stay here to rest while we repair it?"

Finally, a human figure emerges from one of the houses. He is tall with dark skin and eyes. He smiles, though something nervous swims in his expression.

We haven't seen any outsiders here since we hid away...

He clasps Maeve's hand in greeting as he appraises our little group. I cringe. Maeve could be forming that connection to take him over right now. All she needs is an instant, and then she can use him at will. A terrible abuse of such a friendly gesture. "Welcome to Wren. You say there was a storm?"

Maeve's eyes shine. "Yes, it was terrible. We just thought we'd do some fishing on the lake and, well, we ended up here.

We didn't even know there was an island out here!" She laughs, and the man's expression softens a little.

"I'm Henrick. You can stay here while we help you repair your boat."

Other people begin to come out of the nearest meeting lodge where Henrick came from. Curiosity is a dangerous thing. But not as dangerous as Maeve.

They begin to make introductions, but with at least two dozen people living here, I don't catch them all. A woman dressed in blue with piercing violet eyes is Clariss. Another woman with hair as pale as mine and eyes as blue as the ocean is Marena. A kindly older man with peppered brown hair is Drayce. Then the rest begin to blur. But Maeve surveys each one keenly.

She meets my eyes for a moment, and one look in her mind makes me wince.

You will help me determine who the soul summoner and the gift giver are.

I don't respond, but I know this is where I must draw the line. I can't do this for her. If she uncovers that, all is lost.

"Come, join us for lunch," says Atalia, a tall woman with light brown skin and gray hair.

"Thank you," Maeve says, smiling. "You're very kind."

I peek into Atalia's head as she exchanges a glance with Henrick.

I wonder if there's more to this unexpected visit than the stranger says, she thinks, and I want to cheer. I don't dare reveal my talent to them, but I'm relieved they're on their guard. All this time away from society hasn't dulled the sharp edge of their suspicion.

We follow them into the lodge. A dark cloud hangs over me, and my chest feels tight and itchy. This morning's ordeal has taken a toll on me. I couldn't save my friends, but hopefully I can save these people from my mother.

The inside of the lodge is an expansive room with door-ways on each of four sides that likely lead to smaller rooms. The center is lined with many tables, but the gathered people only fill a handful of them.

"Are there more of you?" I ask impulsively, and Maeve gives me a sharp look. I don't feel any more minds than those in this room, but if all or most of these people are talented, who knows what they might be able to do.

Clariss shakes her head. "It's just us."

"How did you come to live on this island, anyway?" Maeve asks as a cold luncheon of meats and cheese and fruit is passed around.

"We've been here for…a very long time," Henrick says carefully. "This area flooded long ago, and we're all that's left of the inhabitants."

The only ones to survive that monster's treachery, he thinks sadly. This confirms that these, or at least most of them, are the original party that was traveling with the soul summoner when Lady Aisling first arrived in Wren. One of them is definitely a life bringer. But who?

"How do you manage to get ashore for supplies in all that fog? Is it always like that?" Maeve is very smart. She's asking all the questions one would expect someone who knew nothing about these islanders to ask. She's doing her best to make them feel comfortable letting down their guard. And if the thoughts in their minds are any indication, it's starting to work.

"We have everything we need right here on the island. There's no need for us to leave." A young man named Tarren says.

"Oh really?" Maeve says. "Do you grow all your own food here too?"

"Yes," says Odeletta, a woman about the same age as Tarren. "Tarren here is our...gardener. He is very good at what he does." She smiles, but some of the others, namely Henrick and Clariss, look a little concerned.

Strangers don't need to know any of our talents, even the simpler ones like our green grower, thinks Clariss.

Drayce interrupts before Odeletta can speak again. "We have all that we need between that and what the lake provides." He smiles, too, but something swims underneath it. Caution.

The others don't miss a beat. "Yes, we're well taken care of. And it's beautiful here," Clariss says.

"That certainly is true," Maeve agrees.

Henrick frowns at Melanthe, who has been staring at her food. "Are you all right?"

Suddenly she smiles. "Oh, yes, of course. I'm just tired from the journey. Getting caught in a storm wore me out."

Maeve is talking through her, of course. A sickening display, but convincing for the islanders. After that, Maeve does a better job making Natasha and Melanthe act more normal. If I couldn't sense her talent pulling their strings, she might have fooled even me.

When lunch is over, we're shown to a little house where we can stay for the night and then Henrick, Tarren, and Marena offer to help us repair our boat. Maeve leaves Melanthe and Natasha behind to settle in but brings me with her. She doesn't trust leaving me alone for a second.

When we reach the little cove where we left the boat, I'm surprised to see the hull is now damaged. The other talented people my mother brought with us are nowhere to be found. No wonder Maeve left a few on the shore; they were here to damage the boat to provide our cover story.

I find them easily, hiding in the woods just out of sight. They're as alarmingly still and silent as ever.

Tarren gasps when he sees the boat. "How did that happen?"

Maeve shrugs. "We must have hit something in the water, or the storm threw something at the boat. It was hard to tell with all the noise and commotion."

Tarren and Henrick gape at her, but Marena's eyes narrow slightly.

There are no large rocks in the lake, Marena thinks. *I should know, I made it.*

So Marena is their water wisher. Hers is the grief that drowned Wren and made my home so hard to find.

They hoist the boat on their shoulders and set it on top of a cart they brought with them. Then we take it back to the village for repair. I can't help but notice that Maeve touches Marena and Tarren at some point.

Now she's ready to use them at a moment's notice. I swallow hard. For the hundredth time today, I wish I had some obsidian with me. If I want to warn the villagers, I'm going to have to find a way to free my friends from Maeve's control. And I need to do it before Maeve has touched them all.

CHAPTER SIXTEEN

They spend the better part of the afternoon repairing our boat. Then we join them for dinner. Maeve grows restless at my lack of progress. All I know so far is that Marena is the water wisher and Tarren is the green grower.

When we retire to our little cottage, Maeve whirls on me the moment the door closes. "Well? Who is it?"

"I don't know yet," I say.

"I don't believe you." Her expression hardens.

"They don't think about their talents all the time." I shrug helplessly. If they did, it would make knowing who to warn much easier.

Maeve sighs with exasperation. "Fine. I'll just have to do this the hard way."

What a hassle. Taking them over one by one and testing their talents will take longer than I'd hoped. And increase the odds of getting caught...

She gives me a sideways glance. "Are you trying to see my plans?"

My eyes widen innocently. "I was just admiring the color of your hair in the candlelight."

Maeve laughs. "You're a terrible liar. Get some sleep. We'll leave this place behind soon enough."

Obediently, I lay down on the small bed in the front room of the cottage, while Maeve exits out the back door. It's no use trying to sleep. My mind won't stop worrying.

I can't let my mother do this.

Melanthe keeps watch—silently staring at me—while Natasha sleeps on the floor in a bedroll. If I can get one of them out from under Maeve's thumb, I might stand a chance at success. Maeve wouldn't dare hurt both girls because she wants to use one as a vessel for her other daughter, the sister I have no memory of. Then I could warn the villagers without worrying about Maeve taking it out on them.

And if I can't, then I'm as doomed as the rest of our friends.

I choke down the sob that wells in my throat. Then I get to work on Melanthe.

This time, the layers of Maeve's power peel away a little faster. I've gotten better with practice.

Melanthe, can you hear me? I say down the tunnel to her mind. At first I get no reply, but I keep working, burrowing under my mother's magic. I try over and over. Finally, she hears me.

Simone, is that you? My friend sounds terrified, and I don't blame her. Her fate scares me too.

I'm here. I'm trying to reach you. Maybe I can help you find your way back up. Throw off Maeve.

She's too powerful. She'll control you too, Melanthe thinks.

I have to risk it. She must be stopped. I need your help to do it.

I've heard of some talented folks who can make their magic tangible, like Emmeline the shadow weaver. I've seen her do it, was even trapped by her shadow ropes once. My talent may be mind-based, but perhaps I can move things too. Like dragging up Melanthe's mind to overthrow Maeve. I have no choice but to try it.

I keep delving deeper, hoping I can find my own way back.

The two of us lost in here won't help anyone. Melanthe's voice gets louder each time I call to her. I'm almost there. And then I see it, the shape of her mind, warm and kind, yet cold and terrified. I stretch my talent toward it and latch on with all my might as I retrace my path back up.

Are you still there? I ask.

Yes, Melanthe's voice is filled with amazement. *I can almost feel my limbs again.*

Are you ready? I don't know how this will work, but you may need all your strength.

Ready as I'll ever be, she answers.

I give one final yank with my magic, and Melanthe's mind suddenly fills the upper regions, shoving Maeve's magic out. I pull my talent back, hoping Maeve doesn't notice she's no longer holding the reins.

Melanthe breathes deeply, then sags into a chair. Tears brim in her eyes as she stares at me across the lone candle lighting the room.

She's free. For now at least. If we can find some obsidian, we can keep her that way.

But there are more pressing things at the moment. *She's*

already out there, I think to Melanthe, *looking for the soul sum-moner and gift giver. She plans to take the villagers over one by one to test their talents.*

Melanthe gets to her feet, a determined look in her eyes, even though she sways unsteadily. *Then we'll stop her.* She glances out the window of the little cottage. Only a few others have candles burning in the windows.

Can you sense where Maeve is? she asks.

I hunt for the familiar feel of my mother's mind. *Odeletta's cottage. So far she's only ruled out her and Tarren. He's a green grower, and she's their youth keeper.*

Melanthe moves to open the front door, but I stop her. *Maeve isn't the only one we need to look out for. She has servants stationed in the shadows near here. We'll have to leave more cautiously.*

Out the back?

I nod. I don't feel any people in that direction.

We creep out the back as quickly and quietly as we can. The night is dark and moonless. Occasionally some fog from the lake creeps by, winding around our ankles before floating away again. Maeve's burgeoning frustration weighs on me every time I check her thoughts. It swells through the village in a way only I could ever detect. Now she's heading for Henrick and Clariss's cottage.

When we pass Odeletta's house I peek in the window. She's passed out on the floor, her pretty hair spread out behind her. Her mind is a jumble of confusion. My hands ball into fists. I want to help her, but I have to deal with my mother first. She's leaving a path of destruction and broken minds in her wake.

We hurry on to warn Henrick and Clariss. Maeve doesn't suspect that Melanthe and I are free. She's so consumed with her task that she hasn't noticed. Which is good, because we need all the luck on our side that we can get.

Suddenly I halt, gripping Melanthe by the arm. My heart thrums like a hummingbird in my chest.

I swear I just felt a familiar mind. One that can't possibly be here.

Sebastian.

CHAPTER SEVENTEEN

My breath stutters as my talent grabs on to the mind of my lost friend.

Simone! Simone! Are you here?

"What is it?" Melanthe asks.

I can hardly speak. I'm shocked. Terrified to believe it's real and not some sort of trick. Finally I find my words again. "Sebastian," I whisper. "Somehow, the storm didn't drown him after all."

A rush of joy floods me. *I'm here in the village. I'm trying to stop Maeve. She's gone after the soul summoner. Where are you?* I swallow hard. *Are you alone?*

Rachel, Jemma, and Kalia are with me. Natasha...she disappeared... We lost her.

No, you didn't! Maeve stole her. She's here, but she's under Maeve's spell again.

Relief fills Sebastian's thoughts, warm and familiar. *Thank goodness for that. We just spotted the village from the forest. We're on our way to you.*

Be careful. Maeve's servants are everywhere. I don't know how many of the people here she's already taken over, but at least two, probably more. And she had half a dozen servants with her when we arrived.

We'll be on our guard.

Does Rachel still have some obsidian? Or did she lose it all in the storm?

Let me check, Sebastian thinks. Moments later, he thinks her reply back to me. *Yes, she does. She lost a couple pieces, but she has some left.*

I breathe out in relief.

Good. We'll need them all. I've got Melanthe with me. I figured out how to throw off Maeve's talent with some effort.

Really? I can hear the surprise in Sebastian's voice. *That's incredible.*

I can't help smiling. *I wasn't sure it would work, but I had to try something. That's why we need the obsidian quickly. I don't want Maeve to take her over again.* My hands suddenly quiver. *Maeve already took mine from me, otherwise I'd give it to Melanthe.*

I can sense Sebastian's dismay. *We'll be there soon.*

Good. I take a deep breath. *And Sebastian?*

Yeah?

I'm really glad you're alive.

He laughs in his mind, and maybe on the outside, too, but I can't see that. *Me too.*

We wait quietly in the darkness while I guide our friends toward our hiding place. I can hardly believe this is real and not some hallucination. It is all in my head, after all. I half expect them not to show and for Melanthe to think I've gone over the edge. Every now and then, I check on my mother to ensure she doesn't find the soul summoner before it's too late. I cross my fingers that it's not Henrick or Clariss because she's about to enter their cottage. She shook hands with Henrick, but I'm not sure about Clariss. Hopefully she'll need to look for an opening to get closer to her, and that will buy us the time we need.

It isn't long before familiar shadows move through the

village. It takes everything I have not to run to my friends and hug them all fiercely.

When Sebastian is close enough, I throw my arms around his neck. He hugs me back, laughing quietly. Jemma and Rachel put their arms around us both, too, while Kalia greets Melanthe. Relief is palpable in the air, but it doesn't last long enough.

I disentangle from my friends' embrace. *We must stop Maeve before it's too late,* I think at all of them at once. *She's in a cottage a little ways over there.* I point to a structure about four houses up the little street. *She's looking for the soul summoner and gift giver, and I'm not sure who they are yet. The people here are very kind. I don't want them to get hurt too.* I wring my hands together.

"First things first," Rachel whispers. "We need to get some obsidian on Melanthe." She rummages around in her bag until she finds what she's looking for: a thin chain with a black rock suspended at the end.

Melanthe frowns, confused. "Why do I need that?"

I pat her shoulder. "It's protection. Maeve can't take you over if you're wearing it. So, keep it on always."

Rachel secures the necklace around Melanthe's neck. "Thank you," she says.

I tug Rachel's sleeve. "Might I have one too? Maeve took mine, and I'm not sure where it is now."

Her eyes widen. "Of course." She digs another obsidian out of her bag and I secure it around my own neck. Suddenly, I feel safer than I have all day.

"What's Maeve's plan, Simone?" Jemma asks.

"She wanted me to help her figure out who the soul summoner and gift giver are, but I wasn't fast enough. She's taking over each villager to test their magic until she discovers what each of them can do."

Jemma's expression hardens. "And then she'll keep all of them under her control afterward, just to have in her pocket."

My heart sinks. I wish she wasn't right.

"Then we need to find her before she gets another dangerous talent under her thumb," Rachel says, stealing a glance at Melanthe.

Melanthe straightens up. "I can keep her restrained as long as necessary. I'll gladly do it."

"Be careful," I warn. "She has a storm brewer in her thrall, and several other talented folks she brought with us hiding on this island and waiting to do her bidding. I don't know what they all do."

"They're either useful or dangerous," Sebastian says. "She wouldn't just take them without reason."

"Then we'll just have to be even more on our guard," Jemma says.

"We do have one other problem we need to consider," Rachel says, and Jemma sighs. "We don't have a boat anymore. Ours was destroyed, and we only got here by using the wreckage to stay afloat while we swam to shore. We need another way off this island."

"Do you know where Maeve's boat is?" Sebastian asks hopefully.

I cringe. "Yes, but it isn't going to help you much. She had her servants damage it so that the villagers would be more willing to help us. Her story was that we got caught in a storm and arrived accidentally."

"Where is it now?" Kalia asks.

"It's somewhere here in the village. Maybe near the meeting-house in the center? They worked on it this afternoon and were planning to finish fixing it tomorrow."

Kalia grins. "I might be able to fix it tonight so we can use it to make a clean getaway."

"You can?" Rachel looks at her surprised.

She shrugs. "I come from a family of sailors. I know boats."

"If that's the case, why don't we split up?" Jemma suggests. "Some of us can find the boat and fix it, and the rest thwart Maeve."

"Good idea," Rachel says. "Why don't you and Kalia and Sebastian look for the boat?"

"No!" Sebastian hisses. "I'm not leaving Simone." He grabs my hand and squeezes. "She might need me."

"He *is* very useful," I say. "What if we need him to take one of Maeve's memories?"

Rachel sighs. "All right, just Jemma and Kalia after the boat then."

We split up and I lead my party toward the cottage where Maeve is setting a trap for Clariss. I touch on all the minds inside and recoil when I feel Henrick's. Maeve has already latched on to him. She's discovered his talent is life bringing. While I'm saddened to see she's controlling him, I'm relieved that he's not one of the ones she needs.

She's been trying to find an excuse to touch Clariss, just for a moment, so she can form that connection and find out what her talent is. But Clariss is both baffled and suspicious as to why this strange woman decided to call on them this late in the evening. Clariss has also noticed that Henrick isn't acting like himself, but right now she's chalking it up to irritation at Maeve.

Surrounding the little cottage is a row of bushes we can use for cover. We're close enough to hear their voices through the open window.

"It's getting late," Clariss finally says, a hint of annoyance in her voice. "We usually retire by this time of the evening."

"Oh!" Maeve exclaims. "I'm so sorry, look at the time. I wasn't even paying attention." *If I can just get her to shake my hand on the way out...*

A chill creeps over my spine. We can't let Clariss fall into Maeve's hands just for being polite. I must do something. My eyes are wide and terrified, and Sebastian notices.

What is it, Simone? he thinks at me.

Maeve is trying to trick Clariss into shaking her hand. I ball my own hands into fists. *I have to warn her.*

Before Sebastian or anyone else can stop me, I sprint for the front door.

CHAPTER EIGHTEEN

I throw the door open, yelling for my mother. "Maeve!
Stop!"

Fire flares in her eyes, but she quickly regains her
calm demeanor. A shiver of magic washes over my body as she
tries to use her talent on me.

If I wasn't wearing the obsidian, I'd be doing her bidding
right now. Probably apologizing to Clariss and Henrick for
barging in like this.

But instead Maeve's expression turns into a deep frown
tinged with surprise, and mine turns into a small smile of relief.

Clariss draws near. "My goodness, Simone, what's
wrong?"

I point at my mother. "She's a body walker. Don't let her touch you."

Clariss's mouth drops open, but she doesn't recoil as I expected.

"Thank you for the warning. We've known body walkers in the past. They've never bothered us before." Clariss eyes Maeve appraisingly.

Maeve puts her hands firmly on my shoulders before I can dodge her. None of my wriggling helps. "Simone is a very imaginative child, I'm afraid. The other day she accused me of being a mountain lion. Can you believe it?" She laughs. Henrick nods along and Clariss smiles uneasily.

"You don't understand. I'm not making this up. She's looking for a gift giver and a soul summoner, who she tracked to this island. She's desperate to bring her family back to life."

This time Clariss takes a step back. There's no doubt in my mind—or Maeve's—that she's one of the talented people we're searching for.

Maeve squeezes my shoulders tighter. "I have no idea what she's talking about," she says, but this time they're not so eager to believe her.

"We'll hear her out, thank you," Clariss says in a clipped tone. "Simone, what does she need a gift giver for, exactly? That talent can't bring back a lost life."

Before I can speak, Maeve clamps a hand over my mouth. "You don't need to hear her lies. It's ridiculous the things she comes up with sometimes."

I flail, but she's much stronger than I've ever given her credit for being.

"Now, listen here, let the girl go!" Clariss says. She glances at Henrick, clearly confused as to why he doesn't object too.

A familiar voice rings out behind me. "She's telling the truth!" Sebastian shouts. "Maeve wants to use your talents for evil so she can bring her children back to life."

Maeve hisses. "They're lying. This is some invention of their imagination. A game they're playing."

"Then why are you so desperate to prevent Simone from speaking?" Clariss says, her voice trembling.

Maeve's eyes go wide and wild. She heads for the door, only to find Rachel blocking her path. Without warning, she shoves me into Rachel, then lurches forward to grab Clariss by the wrist. Clariss tries to wrench her arm out of Maeve's grasp, but Henrick is there, under Maeve's thrall, to hold her fast. It only takes seconds for Maeve to form the connection she needs. Then she releases Clariss's hand and barrels out the door, grappling for a moment with Rachel as she tries to stop her. Maeve manages to get past them, then freezes.

It looks as though she's suspended in thin air. Melanthe enters the cottage, Maeve's body held stiff as it floats back inside.

"You will *not* hurt these people," Melanthe spits every word.

Rachel wastes no time. She springs toward Clariss, pushing an obsidian into her palm, and one into Henrick's too. Her back is to Maeve and she whispers softly enough that my mother won't hear, "It will protect you. Keep it on. Always, or she could take you over at any time now that she's formed a connection with your mind."

Clariss looks alarmed, though she nods unsteadily, shoving the obsidian amulet in her pocket.

Henrick blinks, then sways on his feet. "What? Who? I don't…" When he falls to his knees, Clariss and Rachel move to help him.

"Maeve had him under her control. It's a side effect," I explain.

"Then we should get him somewhere safe," Clariss says. She and Rachel help him onto a couch, and he lies there, mumbling and moving his head side to side.

Then Clariss turns back to us. "I appreciate your help, but who are all of you? And more importantly, how on earth did you get here?"

We exchange a look. "It's a long story," I say. "But the short version is that we came here to stop Maeve."

Clariss frowns. "But you arrived *with* Maeve."

"She captured me." I scuff my toe on the floor. "She's my mother. You used to know her too, actually. We were your neighbors, long ago, when this place was called Wren. Lady Aisling stole us away."

Clariss's mouth drops open. "You mean, Maeve is really Romana?"

I nod. "Yes, but she had an illusion crafter disguise us before we entered the village so you wouldn't recognize us."

"That is very troubling indeed," Clariss says, sitting on a chair next Henrick. "The Romana we knew would never do such a thing."

"Years in the Lady's garden will change a person," Melanthe says.

Clariss frowns. "That explains two of you. Who are the rest of you?"

Rachel speaks up. "We followed to rescue Simone and keep Maeve from carrying out her plans."

"What exactly are those plans?" Clariss asks.

I open my mouth to explain, but before I can say a word, a horrible sound erupts, and the house rattles.

"What was that?" Sebastian grabs my hand and I squeeze it.

Melanthe glances out the door, then she's blown backward, landing in the middle of the room. It breaks her concentration for just a moment, but it's enough for Maeve to be released from her magic hold. She hits the floor and bolts out the door.

"Quick!" I whisper to Clariss. "Who are the soul summoner and gift giver? Those are the talents she wants. We must protect them!"

She sighs. "I'm the gift giver. Drayce is the soul summoner."

"Then we must get to him before Maeve," Rachel says.

Melanthe gets to her feet, dazed. "What *was* that?" she asks.

I shake my head. "Maybe the storm brewer? Maeve has a bunch of talented servants. She's hidden them on the island, but now she may be calling them to her aid."

Sebastian shivers. "That's the one who sank our boat?"

I nod, staring at my feet. I wish I'd been able to stop the storm brewer, but Maeve was too strong.

"We're wasting time standing here." Melanthe marches out the door, and we follow.

When I step outside, I gape. The sky has darkened, roiling with menacing clouds. Wind whips through my white hair, sending the strands back into my face and blurring my vision. The trees bend so far that I fear they might snap in half. The terrible howling wind roars in my ears.

I clutch my cloak around my frame, then reach out for the storm brewer's mind. It takes a few moments, but I locate the feel of Maeve's talent in action at the edge of the village. She's focusing his magic on the cottage we stand in front of.

I quickly tell the others.

"We should raise the alarm," Clariss says. "We never really thought it would come to this, but we put a warning bell in place a long time ago just in case." She glances nervously back at the cottage where Henrick is resting.

"I'll take care of the storm brewer and the alarm," Melanthe says. "Just point me in the right direction."

Rachel hands her a piece of obsidian. "Take this."

Melanthe pockets it, then hurries away at Clariss's direction. While she does her best to take control of the storm brewer by force and raise the alarm, we follow Clariss to Drayce's cottage. By the time we reach his home, the winds have settled and relief courses through us all.

Clariss moves to knock, but I put a hand on her arm. "Let me make sure he's still himself so there are no surprises."

She pulls her hand back. All I can feel is the shape of Drayce's mind sleeping peacefully.

"I think it's safe. He's sleeping."

Clariss knocks loudly, and in a minute or two Drayce answers the door, yawning. "What's going on?" he asks, his eyes widening as he takes in the sight of all of us before him.

"May we come in? It's important. Gravely important," Clariss says.

Her tone leaves no room for argument, and he holds the door wide. We file in quickly and quietly, and I close the door behind us. My talent locates Maeve on the other side of the village, trying to determine what yet another villager's talent is.

That's when the bells begin to ring. That must be what the

curious tower in the center of the village is for. A way to warn everyone at once.

I only hope too many aren't already Maeve's. At least we've reached the ones she needs most first.

As Clariss tells Drayce about Maeve and her plans, his face drains of color and he sinks into the nearest chair.

"She's a body walker? You're certain?" he asks. "And it's really Romana? I can't believe she'd do this."

"Definitely," I say. "I'm a mind reader. I know what body walking feels like. I've witnessed her mind in other people's bodies. And everything we've uncovered so far confirms she's my mother."

Drayce and Clariss both shiver.

"That's horrible," he says. I can only nod my agreement.

Drayce gets to his feet. "We need Marena, and Atalia too. They might be able to help us fight Maeve if it comes to that."

Sebastian looks at him quizzically. "What can they do?"

Drayce smiles. "Marena is our water wisher. And Atalia is an earth rattler."

Hope springs in Sebastian's thoughts. And mine too. Water wishing may sound like a basic talent at first, but it's really quite formidable if put to creative use. And an earth rat-tler can literally knock you off your feet. As long as Maeve doesn't have them under her spell already, they will be most helpful.

I reach out for her mind again, sensing her frustration and growing rage that the villager she just took over is not who she needs. She's also frustrated that Dasco is no longer responding to her demands. Melanthe must have been successful in both her tasks.

Suddenly, Maeve realizes, thanks to one of her spies, that we're no longer at Clariss and Henrick's cottage. Her servants begin to search the village.

It won't be long before she finds us.

"Maeve knows we've moved. She'll find us soon," I tell the others.

We step outside as other confused villagers begin to appear in the doorways of their cottages.

"What's happening, Clariss?" Marena asks as she hurries over.

Clariss takes her hands. "A body walker has come for me and Drayce. It's Maeve. We must defend ourselves against her.

She has servants with talents under her control hidden all over this island."

Marena recoils, then her hands ball into fists at her sides. "We won't let her take you, that's for certain."

"We should get Azalia too," Drayce says, just as the woman rounds the corner and approaches our group. "There she is."

Rachel passes out obsidian to all who don't yet have one, while Clariss and Drayce explain the situation. They've hardly finished before a new smell wafts through the air.

Smoke.

Melanthe sprints up the road from the tower, closely followed by Jemma, Kalia, and a now-free Dasco floating along in front of them, half-conscious.

"Fire!" she shouts.

We glance up just as flames engulf the bell tower in the center of the village. Wood creaks and groans, and the fire pops and snaps. The structure sags, then collapses in on itself, rattling our bones and ears with the resounding clang of the bells hitting the ground.

CHAPTER NINETEEN

Horror trills over me like ants marching across my skin. Maeve brought a fire breather with her.

Now *that* is a dangerous talent.

While the flames consume the remains of the tower and begin to spread to the closest cottages, Maeve's servants march up the road toward us.

I don't know what any of them do. And that terrifies me.

Maeve's mind inside them is focused and intent on keeping us away from her while she continues her hunt. One of the girls, the redhead I believe Maeve called Margareta, stops and opens her mouth. Fire flickers on her tongue. She breathes out, sending a plume of flames in our direction. Our group scrambles back toward one of the cottages. They're made of stone, but the roofs are thatched.

Which might become a problem.

Marena, however, immediately counters the girl's attack with her own. Water bursts from the earth, dousing the fire breather and her flame. It only serves to make Maeve angrier.

"Maeve's coming," I whisper.

Rachel puts her hand on my shoulder and squeezes. "We won't let her take them."

The fire breather still approaches, only temporarily dissuaded by Marena's blast of water. Maeve isn't done with Margareta's talent either. She lets loose an even larger tongue of flame, setting cottages on both sides of the street alight.

Jemma reaches me and Sebastian and grips both of our arms tightly. "Run and hide. Simone, stay on top of whoever comes near you so you'll know when to keep moving. Keep each other safe."

I've never been a fighter in a physical sense. My greatest strength has always been my mind and my talent. But I tried standing up to my mother twice now, and each time I've failed. Jemma is probably right. We should run and we should hide.

I glance over at Sebastian and think at him, *I don't think I'm ready to give up and run yet.*

Sebastian grips my hand tightly. *Neither am I.*

I turn to Jemma. "We can still be helpful. I promise we won't get in the way. Only I can tell you what Maeve is thinking."

Jemma bites her lip and looks like she's about to say something. Rachel puts a hand on her shoulder. "She's not wrong."

Jemma nods and sighs. "Fine. But if things go sideways, you two need to get out of here and get help."

We nod and face Maeve's approaching servants. I shudder as I prod their minds. Maeve's grip on them is very strong. I might be able to pry it off each of them like I did with Melanthe, but that will take time we don't have. I hear their cries of despair, their lost thoughts swirling in a sea of confusion somewhere deep within.

We all form a circle around Drayce and Clariss. Melanthe yanks Margareta off her feet with her magic while Marena sends a gush of water in her direction. Her flames don't ebb. Instead the water hisses and steams. Maeve glares down at us through her eyes. Another of her servants appears on the road and raises his arms—my stomach turns when I realize it's Tarren—and the woods come alive. Trees creak and groan, their branches stretching and elongating toward us at a terrifying speed.

"Green grower!" I cry, as a huge branch sweeps through our group, breaking our formation and sending us flying in all directions. Dazed, I struggle to get to my feet, but it's harder than usual. I think I hit the stone wall of a cottage. Sebastian lays motionless beside me. My heart twists, but I quickly check and see he is still breathing. That's a relief at least.

Melanthe and Atalia are already on their feet and engaged with holding back Maeve's dangerous servants, dodging fire and trees and vines. Frantically, I seek out Marena. She's several feet away, lying on the ground. I reach for her mind, and find it dazed and slumbering, far, far away. Rachel groans nearby, and I catch a glimpse of Clariss's shoes off to my right. I send my talent wide.

I need to know where Maeve is now. I don't know how long I was unconscious or how far she's traveled since I last checked.

I suck my breath in sharply when I realize she's here, hidden somewhere close. I'm not quite sure where yet, but close enough that I worry for Drayce and Clariss's safety. This time

when I try to get to my feet, I succeed. Sebastian is still unconscious, so I go to Rachel and help her up.

"Maeve's here. She's watching, waiting for an opportunity
to take them." Rachel nods, and goes to Clariss. Drayce is awake
now and by Marena's side, trying in vain to rouse her. Blood
trickles from the side of her head.

Without her, we can't hope to hold back the fire breather
for long.

The thought makes my knees weaken.

I can't see Maeve, but I can feel the presence of her mind
like someone breathing down my neck. Drayce looks at me
helplessly. "She won't wake up," he whispers. I just stare at him. I
have no idea what to say.

Maybe I can help her. Maybe I can bring her mind to the
surface. There's no magic suppressing it, but it's lost in there
all the same. But I'll need to concentrate and that will be difficult with the battle raging nearby. The third servant is doing…
something, though I'm not sure what. I frown as I realize it
looks like the ground moves, but just around her feet. Then I
realize what it is.

Spiders.

She's a spider caller. I shudder. I've heard of those, but never met one. I don't know what you'd use it for, unless you're someone like Maeve who wants to scare others.

When the spiders rush toward us, I use my talent to communicate with them. Spider minds are even simpler than those of rabbits and squirrels and birds, more droning and determined and single-purposed. The spider caller's magic has turned them on us, but I convince them we're friends and don't wish to hurt them. Give them the feeling that we're not dangerous, not a threat, and that they can pass by us, leaving us untroubled. To my relief, they give us a wide berth, then circle back to the spider caller. Her mouth drops open. Maeve is surprised by this turn of events. But it won't set her back for long.

The fire breather hasn't stopped for a moment either, nor has the green grower. The ground was shaking intermittently, but now Atalia wrestles with vines circling her and pinning her arms to her sides, almost like that terrible snake we met in the jungle not long ago. But her struggles are in vain. Tarren's grip is strong, and he uses the vines to tie Atalia to a tree. The ground beneath her rumbles, but not enough to shake her loose.

Meanwhile Margareta is becoming more indiscriminate

about where she shoots her flames. Several trees have caught fire, and Tarren uses those against Melanthe as well. My friend throws everything she has at them, but they dodge and weave and continue the attack. Several cottage roofs are now ablaze.

We need Marena. And we need her awake.

I kneel down beside her motionless form. I close my eyes and send my talent into her mind, searching for her, for something to pull up to the surface. A few scattered thoughts flit by me, and I follow them back to their source. She is deep within herself, and I can feel a pulsing pain resonating through her that she hasn't come to terms with yet. If I can do this, it's going to be painful for both of us when she wakes.

Finally I sense something—the distinct shape of a mind, lost, alone, and confused.

I grab onto it with my talent and yank as hard as I can. Marena's mind resists, but I don't let go. I keep pulling with all my might. It's a tug-of-war to bring her back to the surface, to save us from the fire breather and Maeve's evil machinations.

It's also exhausting. I finally begin to gain some ground, but it feels as though I'm trying to draw her up through quicksand. The constant noise and distractions of the battle raging around us doesn't help either. I can hardly hear myself think, let alone Marena.

Fire crackles louder than before and something heavy crashes nearby. I startle, but I don't lose my grip on her mind. I'm almost there. One more tug, and finally Marena's mind rises to the surface. She gasps as her eyes open wide. Pain bursts through her, sending her mind reeling back into unconsciousness. I yank my talent out of her head like I've been burned.

Then I glance up.

We're surrounded by fire. Everywhere I look, something is burning. I get to my feet. Drayce's eyes widen with horror.

"Marena's our only hope," he whispers.

Tears sting my eyes along with the smoke. If Marena is our only hope, then we're already lost. The heat from the fire is searing, and I back up closer to Drayce. My pulse thrashes loudly in my ears.

"I'm sorry, I'm trying to get her to come up, but she doesn't want to yet."

"Can't you tell her what's happening?"

"She won't listen!" Her mind is so unwilling to wake that nothing I think toward her will reach her through unconsciousness.

Simone! Where are you? Sebastian's and Rachel's thoughts scream for me.

I'm with Marena and Drayce! We're trapped!

I feel more than hear the terror in Sebastian's mind. He can't quite put to words his fear of losing me. I feel the same way about him. We're family. We need each other.

I have to find a way out of this.

I have one idea left.

Mother! I cry out to Maeve as loud as I can make my thoughts. Her mind is roiling with frustration and rage and the single-minded determination to capture the two talents she needs. *Help!*

I can sense her irritation at my intrusion. She doesn't answer my pleas.

Please! I'm trapped by fire. I can't get out of it!

Is this a trick? she wonders. *Are you trying to fool me, Simone?*

I'm not, I swear on my life. I will die if you don't help me!

Hot fear bursts through her, and she pauses her attack to find me visually. She's closer than I realized. I catch sight of her through the flames. Horror fills her thoughts. *Drayce is with you too. I might need him. I should never have left my water wisher on the edge of the lake…*

You should never have been trying to capture other talented people to begin with! The force of my thought makes her take a physical step back. *You're destroying the place that was once our home for NOTHING!*

My mother's servants have stilled, and the glimpses I see of my friends through the ring of fire surrounding us reveal their panicked faces. Rachel shouts something about getting water from the lake to douse the flames. But by then it will be too late.

Your obsession with the family you can't have has destroyed the last piece of it. My fear has solidified into rage. *I'm going to die, and it's all your fault!*

Hot tears sting my face, and smoke begins to fill up my lungs. Drayce coughs too, but Marena is still stubbornly unconscious.

Hopelessness floods my limbs, making my legs weak. I crumple to the ground.

I can no longer see Maeve, but the despair in her voice is palpable. *Simone, I'm so sorry, I had no idea, I never meant for this to happen…*

Suddenly a great wind rises up, beating down the flames nearest to me until they're smothered. The wind whistler under her control, no doubt.

Then Maeve swoops in, wrapping her arms around me, crying.

I'm so sorry, I'm so sorry, I'm sorry...

CHAPTER TWENTY

The spell is broken, and Maeve releases her hold on her servants. Rachel wastes no time rounding up the others and ensuring anyone talented is wearing obsidian. My mother cups my face in her hands.

"Losing you again is the last thing in the world I ever intended to do." Tears stream down her cheeks. "I got so focused on getting you *all* back… You tried to tell me, and I wouldn't listen. I'm so sorry."

I don't know what to say. I'm relieved, but also overwhelmingly sad and angry that this is what it took to bring her to her senses.

I hug her instead of speaking. And I don't open my talent

to her mind either. I already know how she feels. It's leaking out of every pore.

"Maeve...or Romana as we once knew you," Drayce says. "We're going to have to arrest you."

Now that the fire has been put out, we're surrounded by the villagers. All of them wearing obsidian in some form. It's really over.

"What will happen to her?" I ask Drayce as he and Atalia lift Maeve to her feet and bind her hands.

"We have a cottage we can use as a jail for now. We'll have to meet as a village and decide how to deal with her on a more permanent basis."

A sudden dread strikes me. "You...you won't hurt her, will you?"

Clariss puts a hand on my shoulder. "No, we'll just...prevent her from doing more harm. That's all."

I breathe out in relief. Sebastian appears at my side, and it's such a comfort that I throw my arms around him. He hugs me back. Sometimes, the best of friends don't need words.

We watch silently as the villagers take Maeve away. My insides are still a roil of confused emotions, but mostly I just feel relief. And exhaustion. Though there's a very, very tiny part of me that's a little sad that I'll never get to see my brother or sister or father again.

But it's for the best, for everyone, of that I'm absolutely certain.

The next morning we join the villagers in the common area for breakfast. The villagers who Maeve took over yesterday are mostly themselves again. Sebastian, Kalia, Natasha, and I have been peppering them with questions since the moment we sat down.

I scrunch up my face, confused. "So why were there bread crumbs planted in storybooks and other town records about where you went?" Our first, incorrect path had us heading all the way out to sea—literally.

Marena laughs and Drayce smiles wryly. "We didn't want anyone to find us, so we planted a false trail just to be safe," he says.

Marena playfully tugs his hand. "And you wouldn't have

had to do it if you hadn't been so careless with your journal." His face turns red and he adjusts the collar of his tunic.

"Yes, that was an unexpected complication, I'm afraid."

Sebastian bursts out laughing. "You *lost* the journal?"

"It was the early days, just after Marena had drowned our village. Atalia helped by raising the island from the earth, while the rest of us paired up to get supplies from the nearest villages before we left for the island permanently." Drayce sighs. "I'd mentioned our plans in the last entry of my journal. We didn't know if we'd need to run from the Lady's minions, so we kept all our possessions on us. It must have fallen out of my bag somewhere at the market."

Rachel laughs too. "And later when someone found it, they must have given it to the library thinking it might be important, or even belonged there."

Drayce nods. "Yes, so we took precautions. We couldn't risk the Lady getting her hands on our talents. We weren't sure how she'd managed to steal so many from our village and were afraid of losing the rest of the people we loved if we went after her." He puts his arm around Marena. She has a nasty bruise on her forehead and a few scratches on her face after last night's battle. "And really, as much as we love magic, no one truly needs talents as powerful as ours." He gestures to Clariss, who sits across from him.

Clariss waves him off. "Well, I have to disagree with you there. We never would've survived for so long had I not been able to give just the right talents to the others. Including temporarily making Odeletta a book binder so she could plant stories of our journey in other books."

Odeletta leans in conspiratorially. "Once we realized Drayce's journal was missing, I volunteered. I wanted one last chance to see the three territories before we closed ourselves off from the world." She shrugs. "It wasn't that difficult either. I just visited a library here, a town record keeper there, and when they weren't looking, I used the magic Clariss gave me to add a version of our story."

Jemma's eyes widen in surprise. "Hold on. You gave other people here their talents? You mean you weren't all talented to begin with?"

Clariss shakes her head. "No, just Drayce, Marena, Atalia, and me, actually. When we saw what had become of Wren and how few people remained, we made our plan to create the lake and hide what was left of our village and loved ones on the island. We knew we'd need certain talents to survive. So I gave a few of the others something useful. Tarren became our green grower, Odeletta our youth keeper, after she was done with her book binding duties, of course, and Henrick our life bringer." She frowns. "In hindsight, I suppose I should have given someone a talent that would be better for defending ourselves should the need arise."

"To be fair," Jemma says, "an enormous fog-drenched lake is a pretty good defense. Sounds like it was enough to deter Lady Aisling if she ever realized you were out here."

"I doubt she did," Henrick says. "She hunted down the talented but wasn't much for research herself. She always let others do her dirty work. I can't imagine she ever set foot inside the Archives. It would be far too tedious for her."

I grow more serious. "I believe it. We"—I point to Sebastian, Melanthe, Kalia, Elias, and Natasha—"were all people she used to do that dirty work for her. She'd already taken Maeve, my mother, prisoner from our village and used her body walking talent to force us to help her capture other talented children."

Clariss sighs. "And now Maeve—Romana—has become corrupted in the wake of her grief. Had she come here without this greed in her heart, we would have welcomed her with open arms." She looks directly at me. "And you, Simone. This is your home too. Your real one. I remember you from when you were small. You were always causing Romana trouble. But she loved you and your sister and brother so dearly."

"What happened to them?" I ask. Without warning, my chest aches. I already know they're gone; I'm just not sure how.

Clariss exchanges a look with Henrick. He speaks first. "They were here. For a time. But then your father got the idea in his head that he could rescue the two of you. He begged Clariss to give him a talent. Something powerful enough to end the Lady."

"I refused," she says sadly. "I thought he was going on a fool's errand. That he'd never even get close. We tried to convince him to stay. At least to leave your siblings behind with us. But they were all headstrong and insisted on going. One night, they took a boat and left. We never saw them again."

I stare at my fingers. "So they really are gone." Some part of me had been hoping against hope that Maeve was wrong and we'd find the rest of our family here, alive and well. But that was too much to hope for.

Marena sits next to me and puts an arm around my shoulders. "Simone, your biological family may not be here anymore, but this is your home. You're welcome to remain here as long as you like, and come and go as you please."

Henrick cleared his throat. "Well, there is one thing we will require of all of you before you leave. And that's to keep this place a secret. We just want to live here in peace. And if another body walker or magic eater is born..." He spreads his hands wide, but we all understand his meaning.

"They might want to accumulate power," I say.

Sebastian looks around shyly. "I might be able to help with that. If you want."

Clariss leans closer. "What's your talent?"

I squeeze his hand and he smiles at me. "I'm a memory stealer. But I only do it when someone asks me to or it's absolutely necessary."

Clariss nods. "If all but Simone would submit to having their memories of how to reach this place removed, I think we'd all sleep much better at night."

Jemma and Rachel immediately give their approval, the others more reluctantly so, but agree just the same. We can all see the wisdom in this.

"Thank you," Henrick says. "We appreciate your help in preserving our peace."

"What will become of Maeve?" I ask.

The islanders exchange a look, but Jemma speaks up before they do. "We'd discussed having a talent taker remove her magic permanently."

The islanders instinctively recoil at the suggestion, and Jemma's expression falters. "We alerted the network, so they know there's a body walker out there."

"We have a better solution," Clariss says. "As a gift giver, I can give anyone a talent. If they're already talented, what I give them would take the place of the original talent. I could replace Maeve's with a harmless one. She'd still have magic, but she'd no longer be a threat."

"Yes!" I say, clapping my hands together. "That's perfect." I loathe the thought of stealing my mother's magic entirely.

"The woman we knew was very cautious about her talent. Mostly she only used it as a party trick," Henrick says.

Marena laughs. "Or that one time when she sent a group of bandits on their way. Turned them right around and marched them into the hills. They were so confused by what had happened that they never troubled Wren again."

"Why didn't you use your talent on Lady Aisling?" Rachel wonders.

Clariss's expression turns serious. "I considered that. But I have to touch a person to do it. She would have just taken my talent from me before I could do anything to her. It was much too dangerous."

I nod. Lady Aisling's talent was indeed the most awful and awesome I've ever known.

CHAPTER TWENTY-ONE

The others continue to talk, but my feet grow restless. I get up from the table and begin to wander around the village. It's hard to believe I once lived here, loved it here, and was dying to return. It's lovely, and the people are kind, but it doesn't feel like home in the way I thought it would.

With a start, I realize why: I could stay here, but my friends cannot. I'd have to give them up to live in isolation like this.

And I don't want to do that.

As I told Maeve many times throughout our journey together, Sebastian and the others are my family too. I can't leave them. I'd miss them too much.

But I'll come back to visit my mother and the islanders from time to time. I rather like them, and I want to know Maeve better, especially if she isn't dangerous anymore.

My feet have brought me to the cottage the islanders are using as a prison for her. I pause, uncertain. Should I enter and speak to my mother? Or should I walk on by?

The decision is more difficult than I expected.

In the end, I step inside and find one of the villagers—an untalented one—guarding Maeve, who is shackled to a chair and a support beam. The villager raises an eyebrow, but moves to the far side of the room to give us a few moments to talk.

Maeve looks at me with surprise. "I didn't expect to see you, Simone."

"I wasn't sure I'd come either," I say, sitting in a chair across from her and swinging my legs.

"I just… I want you to know how sorry I am," she says. "Hurting you was never a thing I intended to do."

I frown. "But I told you that you were. Many times. Why didn't you listen to me?"

Maeve shrugs. "I don't know. I suppose I thought I knew best. I should've listened to you. I wish I had."

"Me too."

"Do you know what they plan to do to me?" she asks.

Before I can answer, Clariss appears in the doorway. "Yes, she does. Why don't we tell her, Simone?"

I nod silently, unable to look my mother in the eyes. I know this is for the best, and it's certainly much better than removing her magic entirely, but I'm not sure how she'll feel about it.

Maeve glances between us both, then steels herself by sitting up straighter. "What is it?"

Clariss's expression softens slightly. "We've decided to give you a new talent."

Maeve's eyebrows raise in surprise. "Which one?"

"There will be no more forcibly using other people's bodies. But you will be able to change the color of anything you touch."

Maeve nods slowly, digesting this news. "A color changer." She swallows hard. "Will you do it now?"

"Yes," Clariss says. "We believe it's best to do it now rather than later."

"All right. I'm ready." Maeve's jaw is set, as if bracing for it to hurt.

"Should I leave?" I rise from my chair.

"Only if you wish to," Clariss says.

I look to Maeve. "I'd like it if you stayed, Simone," she says. I reach out to squeeze her hand for a moment. She squeezes back, a look of relief on her face. Then I let go and twist my fingers in my lap instead.

Clariss pulls a chair up next to Maeve and places a hand on her forehead. She closes her eyes as she concentrates on her task. Maeve leans back, but soon tenses as Clariss's magic flows through her. Maeve gasps when Clariss releases her hold on her forehead.

"There," Clariss says. "You are no longer a threat to anyone."

"What will become of me now?" Maeve asks her.

"We have decided that you still must pay for your crimes. But we remember the woman you once were, a valued member of our community. We know Lady Aisling stole many of your memories, but we hope to help you regain some of them. You will remain here as our prisoner for five years. We will treat you well, we swear to that, but you will not be able to leave this cottage or its grounds during that time. At the end of five years, we will revisit whether or not to set you free and welcome you into the community as a full member and with the freedom to wander this island as you please."

Maeve bows her head. "Thank you."

"We understand how grief can twist one's mind. But know this: you will never again leave this island. We cannot risk you returning to Lady Aisling and informing her of this place. It's too dangerous."

Unshed tears shine in the corners of Maeve's eyes. "I'm glad to have found home again. These buildings, they...feel familiar to me. It's right for me to be here."

My heart twists for my mother. And another part of me grieves the fact that I don't feel the same about this place.

I put a tentative hand on my mother's arm. "I don't think I can stay here with you." Her expression droops. "But I'll visit. I promise."

She hangs her head. "I understand."

"I know why you did what you did. It's easy to grasp for false hope when you have nothing left to lose."

"But I took you for granted. I wanted everything back, instead of appreciating the tiny miracle it was that you were still alive. I hope you can forgive me one day."

That word strikes me in an unexpected way. *Forgive.* I'm not sure I've quite forgiven her yet. But I do know I don't want to lose my mother. "I want to know you better. That's why I'll come back to visit."

Clariss stands. "Why don't you start now? Simone, you won't be leaving until the morning anyway. You may remain in this cottage with your mother as long as you like. We can have dinner brought to you both later."

I glance at Maeve. "Yes, I'd like that very much."

Clariss glides out of the cottage. The guard follows her, resuming a post outside instead.

Maeve pats my hand and smiles. "My dear daughter. Let me tell you what I remember of our time here…"

EPILOGUE

I stand at my open window in our cottage in Sebastian's home village. I've finally managed to keep hold of the name—Willworth. A light breeze ripples over me, making the curtains flutter. The earthy scent of freshly turned soil from the farmlands behind the village on one side wafts over me, but all I can see are the wooded streamlands I know and love so well.

We've been back here for two weeks, settling into a new sort of normal. My mother, Maeve, remains imprisoned on the island of Wren. I'll visit her again soon enough, but for now, I'm enjoying my freedom.

It's finally beginning to feel real.

Are you ready? Sebastian thinks at me from downstairs.

I smile even though I'm alone in my room. *Almost*, I think back.

Since our adventures, my hold on my talent has improved. All the minds here in the village are no longer quite so overwhelming.

I head downstairs to join Sebastian and Jemma. I find them by the front door. Jemma is holding a basket filled with sandwiches for our lunch. Sebastian's face lights up when he sees me, and together the three of us leave the house, making our way through the village to the woods.

Once I'm outside in the daylight again, I smile, stretching my arms wide to feel the sun's warmth over my body.

"Are you all right?" Sebastian asks.

"Yes," I say. And for the first time since I can remember, I mean it with all my heart.

The villagers on the streets nod their greetings as we pass by. They still think me odd, but the twinge of fear I used to sense in their thoughts has disappeared. It isn't long before we find ourselves surrounded by the sweet green trees and the mossy banks of the streams. Sebastian and I trace the path of one stream for a little way while Jemma sets out a blanket and our food. Then we sit in a patch of sunlight and have our lunch.

I used to come here to be alone, but now it's much nicer to share it with my friends. My mind wanders over the animals nearby. Slippery fishes swim past, and a den of foxes isn't far away, all nestled together in the hollow of a tree. A mother rabbit and her two babies poke their noses out from under some nearby ferns curiously. Sebastian's eyes widen when he notices them. He and Jemma both go still, not wanting to scare them away.

I greet the rabbits mind to mind, sending soothing images and feelings of safety. Then I hold out a carrot and place it halfway between us and them. The mother takes a tentative step forward and nibbles on it. Moments later, the babies join her, and it isn't long before they eat out of our hands.

Jemma laughs and Sebastian grins.

Their whiskers tickle, he thinks at me. Then I laugh too. True and long and loud.

We're really free now. The Lady has no power and no hope of regaining it. And I found my family, something I'd once believed to be impossible. But the best part is that I finally found a home. It wasn't the one I expected, the one I thought I sought.

But it's the one I chose, and it chose me too.

ACKNOWLEDGMENTS

Sequels are often very strange beasts. They live in your head for so long while writing the first book that putting the words on the page feels both exciting and bittersweet. I've loved living in my mind reader Simone's head for this duology, and I'm so grateful I had the opportunity to share her story.

As always, I must send special thank-yous to those who made this book possible:

My delightful editor, Annie Berger, and the entire, talented Sourcebooks team, but particularly Cassie Gutman, Valerie Pierce, Margaret Coffee, Heather Moore, and Ashlyn Keil. I so appreciate all you do to help my books get into readers' hands!

My fabulous agent, Suzie Townsend, her wonderful assistant, Dani Segelbaum, and the very awesome team at New Leaf Literary & Media.

My family—because this is all for you.

And last but never least, my readers! Thank you so much for taking this journey through the Cometlands with me. I hope you've found some light within these pages.

ABOUT THE AUTHOR

MarcyKate Connolly is a *New York Times* bestselling children's book author and nonprofit administrator who lives in New England with her family and a grumble of pugs. She graduated from Hampshire College (a magical place where they don't give you grades) where she wrote an opera sequel to *Hamlet* as the equivalent of a senior thesis. It was there that she first fell in love with plotting and has been dreaming up new ways to make life difficult for her characters ever since. She is also the author of the Shadow Weaver duology and *The Star Shepherd*. You can visit her online at marcykate.com.